UNDERCOVER ALIENS

CECI JEN[...]

Illustrations by
Michael Broad

ff

faber and faber

First published in 2011
by Faber and Faber Limited
Bloomsbury House, 74–77 Great Russell Street
London WC1B 3DA

Typeset by Faber and Faber Limited
Printed in England by CPI Bookmarque

A CIP record for this book
is available from the British Library

ISBN 978–0–571–26004–1

2 4 6 8 10 9 7 5 3 1

To old friends on distant planets

Read more of Oli and Skipjack's
Tales of Trouble

CONTENTS

New Boy

'Ten-pin bowling,' Skipjack Haynes told Oli Biggles, 'would be a birthday treat. *Revenge of the Phantom Werewolf* in 3D, with popcorn, would be a birthday treat. Going to a science exhibition is *not* a birthday treat.'

'It is when it's my birthday,' said his dad, leading the way up the Town Hall steps.

'D'you know, Dad,' sighed Skipjack, 'sometimes it seems impossible that we're related.'

For although his dad knew exactly where electricity came from and could design a go-kart that reached 25 miles an hour (down Skid Hill with a strong tail wind), Skipjack himself was resolutely non-scientific. He avoided science for the same reason that Superman avoided Kryptonite: he feared it had the power to destroy him. When faced with too much science, Skipjack would screw his eyes shut, clamp his hands over his ears and shout, 'Bibble-bibble-bibble!' until removed. His best friend Oli, on the other hand, quite liked science because it helped you understand why a Bugatti Veyron went faster than a Ferrari Enzo or why, if you dropped Slugger Stubbins and a feather off the top of a tall building, Slugger Stubbins would make a bigger dent.

Fortunately for Skipjack, this science exhibition had lots of things for visitors to try out, things which were such fun that he could forget they had anything to do with science at all. Although they did not, alas, include Slugger Stubbins, a feather and a tall building, they did include a narrow bench onto which were screwed an enormous microphone and a wooden box covered with switches and clips, from which a tangle of copper wires cascaded. Also attached to the bench was a panel of dials and levers, black and shiny, with even more switches spouting even more electric spaghetti.

Skipjack's dad was very excited. 'It's an

antique radio transceiver! Radios are *amazing* things. Did you know that radio waves can travel for thousands of miles into space at the speed of light?'

'In that case,' said Skipjack, 'we'd better send a message to the aliens.' He found a switch marked 'ON' and flicked it down. At first nothing happened and Oli was about to point out that the radio was probably too old to function any more when a faint hissing noise came to their attention. This grew more and more insistent until it was exactly like the very loud hissing noise that Miss Harbottle the librarian always made when Oli and Skipjack giggled during Reading Hour. Both boys looked around in dismay, expecting to find themselves being glared at through green-rimmed spectacles. But Miss Harbottle, if she was hissing at all, was hissing elsewhere. This particular hiss they tracked down to a pair of round speakers set into the wooden panel.

'It works,' said Skipjack. He twiddled a few dials and the hiss turned into a loud electric crackle that made Oli's hair stand on end.

Skipjack leaned in close to the microphone and said, in his best radio voice,

'Hoombinny-squilpok.'

Satisfied, he turned to Oli. 'Just imagine,' he said. 'My words are travelling through the universe at the speed of light.'

'Then it's a pity you didn't say something more interesting,' Oli told him. '"Hoombinny-squilpok" is a useless thing to say if we want the aliens to visit us – we need to make them think

Planet Earth is a really groovy place, full of things they'd love.'

'Such as?'

'Prawn-cocktail crisps,' replied Oli. '*Top Gear*. The FA Cup. Here, I'll tell them.'

But before he could take the microphone, a strange thing happened. The crackle from the speakers was interrupted by a high-pitched whine and then a faraway voice said, 'Yabbaflibba-boing.'

They stared at the extraordinary machine. 'Did you hear that?' whispered Skipjack. 'I got an answer!'

'Say it again,' urged Oli, forgetting all about prawn-cocktail crisps, *Top Gear*, the FA Cup and the uselessness of Hoombinny-squilpok as an alien call-sign.

So Skipjack put his mouth to the microphone and repeated, 'Hoombinny-squilpok.'

More crackling, another whine, then the tinny reply: 'Yabbaflibba-boing.'

'It's aliens!' gasped Skipjack. 'They're talking to us!'

But his dad, who had been watching all this

with amusement, said, 'At the risk of bringing you back down to earth with a dull thud, I expect it was only the nearest amateur radio enthusiast. You'd be surprised how many people still use these old transceivers, just for fun.'

Skipjack, however, was positive he'd made contact with little green men and, as he went to bed that evening, he resolved to sit up all night and watch out for spaceships. But somehow such resolutions always vanished beneath the weight of his eyelids and he was asleep within minutes, as usual.

The next day was Pocket Money Day for Skipjack, which traditionally meant a visit to Doctor Levity's Joke Shop.

This shop was a treasure trove of magic gizmos and nifty tricks, as well as being home to the many bizarre items that Doctor Levity had collected on his adventures to all corners of the globe, adventures which were often hinted at but never fully described. For Doctor Hamish Levity took great care to retain an air of mystery; he had arrived in the town one day a decade ago and announced quite simply that he was going to open the best joke shop in the galaxy. And so it had happened.

As Skipjack approached the joke shop, with his five-pound note practically jumping out of his pocket with excitement, he saw a boy. It was a boy he had never seen before, and he was gazing into the joke-shop window at a brightly coloured boomerang.

'They're good, those,' remarked Skipjack as he drew up alongside. 'I've had one for ages. They always come back.'

'I'd like one,' said the boy, 'but I haven't got any money.'

'That's usually my problem, too,' nodded Skipjack with sympathy. 'You should have a look inside, anyway. This is the best joke shop in the galaxy.'

The boy looked at him with a strange expression. Then he said, 'I doubt that.' He was about Skipjack's height, with bright green eyes and black hair.

'What's your name?' asked Skipjack.

'Ringo,' said the boy.

'That's a weird name. Mine's Skipjack. Follow me, Ringo.'

He led the way inside. A tall man dressed in purple and topped with a dollop of curly grey hair looked up and beamed.

'Skipjack! My best customer!'

'Hello, Doctor L,' grinned Skipjack. 'And guess what – it's Pocket Money Day.'

Doctor Levity clapped his hands together. 'You mean you'll actually be able to pay? I don't think my heart can stand so much joy.'

Skipjack glanced around the shop and asked casually, 'Is Daisy about?' Daisy was Doctor Levity's granddaughter, who lived with him above the shop and for whom Skipjack had a softish spot: she was very pretty and laughed at all his jokes.

'Afraid not, young Skipjack,' replied Doctor Levity. 'She's gone to buy rabbit food.'

'Ah, well. By the way, this is Ringo,' said Skipjack. 'He'd like a 'rang, but he hasn't got any money.'

Doctor Levity looked at Ringo for a moment. Then he said, 'I'll tell you what, Ringo. If you can make me laugh, or show me something I've never seen before, you can have a boomerang for free.'

Ringo looked back at Doctor Levity. Then, without warning, he waggled his ears. It was not just a mini-waggle of the lobe-tips; those ears flapped so hard they nearly lifted Ringo off the floor and flew him round the room.

While Skipjack stared, open-mouthed, Doctor Levity nodded approvingly. 'That'll do,' he

said. He reached into the window display and removed the boomerang. As Ringo took it he glanced outside.

'My mum and dad are waiting,' he said. 'Thanks.' And he darted out of the shop.

Skipjack watched him run across the street. 'Odd,' he remarked, 'but cool. By the way, Doctor L, I don't suppose you've seen any aliens about today?'

Doctor Levity scratched his woolly head thoughtfully. 'No, not today. Why?'

'Cos yesterday I sent a radio message into space and I got an answer. So now the aliens might be trying to find me. Ah, well. Perhaps Oli was right – I should have told them about prawn-cocktail crisps. Bye.'

'A new family's moved into our road,' Oli's mum said that afternoon over a cup of tea. 'They're renting Mr Jones's house. They've got a boy about your age, Oli. It would be nice if you went round.'

Oli didn't think it would be nice at all. 'He probably knows loads of people already, Mum.

He'll just think I'm a saddo.'

'Actually, he doesn't know anyone,' replied Mrs Biggles. 'They've only just arrived here, from Kalamistan.'

'Kalamistan?' echoed Oli's younger sister Tara as she lowered her biscuit into her mug. 'I thought only sultanas and revolutionaries lived in Kalamistan.'

'Wherever did you get that idea?' wondered her mother. 'And you shouldn't dunk your biscuits.'

'Not even in my own tea?' objected Tara, lifting it out and taking a soggy bite.

'He probably won't even speak English,' grumbled Oli.

'He'll speak a bit, I'm sure,' said Mum. 'Take a football, just in case. Everyone speaks football.'

So a reluctant Oli set off along Pond Lane towards the new family's house. To prolong his journey for as long as possible he did keepie-uppies all the way and when he could no longer avoid arriving he knocked on the front door quietly. Unfortunately his knock was heard and the door opened a crack, through which a

shortish man squinted out. Oli was just thinking
that the squinter didn't look altogether friendly
when the man's dark-brown eyes alighted on the
football Oli was holding and his whole face lit
up. The door was flung open.

'A football!' cried the man in delight.
'Liverpool, Barcelona, AC Milan, Cowdenbeath.
You see? I know all about football. Come in,
come in. I am Mr Kuznet. You must be the son
of the kind lady who visited us earlier today.'

'I'm Oli,' said Oli.

His football-free hand was grasped by both Mr Kuznet's big, squishy paws and squeezed warmly. 'Ringo!' called the man over his shoulder. 'Oli has come to see you, with a football!'

While Oli waited for Ringo to appear, a black-and-white cat slunk down the stairs. It was a small, skinny thing and as it slipped through the kitchen door Oli noticed that it only had three legs. Mr Kuznet followed his glance and said,

'That is our dearly beloved pet, Cuddles.'

'How did he lose his leg?' asked Oli.

'He didn't. He is only supposed to have three legs. It is his breed,' explained Mr Kuznet and then, perhaps because he saw Oli's look of surprise, he added, 'I think they only exist in Kalamistan.'

At this point Ringo arrived and Oli's first thought was how entirely unlike his father the boy looked: tall and thin with vivid green eyes.

'Hi,' he said. 'D'you want to kick a ball around?'

Ringo nodded. 'OK,' he said.

Mr Kuznet beamed. 'This is fine,' he chuckled. 'Bayern Munich, Ajax, Tottenham Hotspur. Long live football.'

The boys went round the house to the back garden. After they had spent a few moments passing the ball wordlessly back and forth, Oli thought he should probably say something, so he asked,

'How long have you been here?'

'We arrived yesterday,' said Ringo.

'Did you fly?'

'Yeah.'

'You're lucky. I've never been in a plane,' said Oli. 'The view must be awesome.'

Ringo frowned. 'Awesome?'

'Amazing,' translated Oli.

Ringo nodded. 'Yeah.'

'Your English is good,' said Oli. 'Did you have lessons in Kalamistan?'

'Er, yeah,' said Ringo.

'My sister Tara says Kalamistan is full of sultanas and revolutionaries. Is that true?'

'Er, yeah. No. Er, I'm not sure.' Ringo looked confused.

Oli couldn't think of anything else to ask after that so they played in silence for a while, until a familiar voice yodelled, 'Ring-go!' and both boys turned round: Skipjack had arrived.

'Hi, Oli!' added Skipjack. 'I called at your house and your mum said you were here. I see you've met Ringo. Show him what you can do with your ears, Ringo.'

Ringo grinned and waggled his ears. Skipjack turned to Oli. 'Cool, huh?'

'Very cool,' agreed Oli. 'But how do you two

know each other?'

'We met in Doctor Levity's. I spent all my pocket money after you left, Ringo – every last penny. I bought some more exploding sweets and another Incredi Ball to add to my collection.' He dug his hand into a pocket and produced a black rubber ball. 'This one's called a Misera Ball – look.' He threw the ball into the air and it let out a mournful wail that grew louder the higher it rose and softer as it came down again.

'That's great,' laughed Ringo.

'You should hear the Laugha Ball – that sounds like a hyena,' said Skipjack. 'Have you used your boomerang yet?'

'Yeah,' said Ringo. 'You were right – it's brilliant.'

Oli frowned slightly. He couldn't help noticing that Ringo was having a much better time now that Skipjack had arrived. This seemed unfair: Oli had come over to be kind because Ringo didn't have any friends and it turned out that Ringo did have a friend after all, who was none other than *his* best friend, Skipjack.

So he was quite pleased when a voice from the

house called, 'Ringo! You must come in now.'

The boys turned to see a woman standing in the back doorway, presumably Ringo's mother although she didn't look much like him either. She had a round face, light brown hair and a worried expression.

'You are still tired from the journey,' she told Ringo. 'You must eat and rest.' Her anxious eyes darted between Oli and Skipjack as she stood on the step, waiting for them to go.

Getting the hint, they said goodbye and walked away. Oli remarked in a low voice to Skipjack, 'There's something a bit dodgy about Ringo.'

'I think he's cool,' said Skipjack.

'Me too,' said Oli quickly. 'I just think there's something a bit dodgy about him. He didn't know much about Kalamistan, for a start, which is where he's supposed to come from.'

Skipjack was throwing his Misera Ball in the air and not really listening any more. 'He should meet Sid,' he said. 'She's been to Kalamistan.'

Sid was an old friend of the boys, a big, jolly woman who ran the local pizza café. She had been an enthusiastic traveller before settling down, and Kalamistan often featured in the memories she shared. Sid would know whether the Kuznets were really from Kalamistan.

'Good idea,' said Oli. 'We'll take Ringo to Sid's place.'

2
The Kalamistan Question

At noon the next day Oli was once again
standing on Ringo's front step, this time with
Skipjack. The door was opened by Mrs Kuznet,
first a tiny crack and then, when she was certain
who the visitors were, a fraction wider, although
she kept one hand on the edge of the door.

'We've come to ask Ringo if he wants to
meet our friend, Sid,' explained Oli. He did not
mention Sid's connection with Kalamistan, in
case Mrs Kuznet detected a Trap and refused
to let Ringo go. (Skipjack did not mention Sid's
connection with Kalamistan either because he
had forgotten all about it and in any case he was
only interested in her connection to pizza.)

Mrs Kuznet looked doubtful. 'Ringo is tired.
I don't think that meeting new people . . .'
she trailed off and looked at the boys in silent

19

desperation, as if wishing they would go away
without her having to ask them to. Just then
Ringo himself appeared.

'Hi, Ringo! Come and have a pizza with us,'
said Skipjack.

Ringo beamed. 'Great. I've heard a lot about
pizza.'

Skipjack looked astonished. 'You mean, you've
never eaten any?'

'Where I come from . . .' began Ringo, but his
mother nudged him and he stopped.

'You shouldn't go without your father's
permission,' she said. 'Wait until he comes back
from the grocery shop.'

'Aw, Mum,' Ringo protested. 'Dad said it was
good for me to make friends.' And, before she
could object further, he picked his jacket off a
chair, ducked under her arm and shot out of the
door.

'Be careful!' Mrs Kuznet called after him.

'Your mum seems to think there's something
dangerous about eating pizza,' remarked Oli.

Ringo reddened. 'She worries,' he sighed.

'They all do,' agreed Skipjack. They reached

the Pond Lane bus stop. 'This is where we wait for the Number 11,' Oli told Ringo.

'We're going on a bus?' Ringo looked as excited about this as he had about the pizza.

'Yeah, but you shouldn't look so happy about it,' said Oli, 'cos the driver will probably be Mr Grimble and he's like something from a Chamber of Horrors.'

'What's a Chamber of Horrors?' asked Ringo.

'Just you wait,' said Skipjack.

The bus drew up and the doors banged open. At the wheel sat a huge ogre of a man, behind a beard so big and bushy it looked as if he was under attack from Baa-baa the Black Sheep.

'See?' muttered Oli. Ringo gulped.

But to their astonishment Mr Grimble beamed them a huge smile, packed with teeth, and said, 'Good morning, boys. How are you today? What a pleasure it is to see you both. And I see you've brought a friend along. Come aboard, come aboard.'

While Oli and Skipjack gawped at him, the bus driver continued to beam. 'I hope you enjoy your journey,' he cooed. 'Have a nice day.'

The man had clearly lost his marbles and everything else besides. The boys edged hurriedly past him and scurried down the aisle to the very back of the bus.

'What was all that about?' Oli wanted to know as he flopped into his seat.

'Beats me,' shrugged Skipjack. 'Either he's gone bonkers or he's had a personality transplant.'

The explanation for Mr Grimble's sudden conversion to sweetness and light was quite simple: the bus company was launching its annual Driver of the Year competition and Mr Grimble was determined to win. He was working hard to secure as many votes as possible from his passengers, but being nice was a terrible strain, especially to the likes of Oli and Skipjack. With every smile that he forced out, Mr Grumble feared his face would crack up. It had better be worth it.

Once the boys were settled in their seats, Ringo slipped from his pocket a small, black gadget with a white screen. He glanced at it briefly and was about to replace it when Oli and

Skipjack, always alert to gadgets, spotted it.

'What's that?' asked Skipjack curiously.

'Just a mobile phone,' replied Ringo.

'I've never seen one like that before,' said Oli. 'It must be really new.'

'It is.'

'My mum won't let me have a mobile phone,' grumbled Skipjack. 'She says I'd just lose it.'

'I'm always losing this,' said Ringo, 'so now I have to pay for replacements.'

'No wonder you didn't have any money for the joke shop,' remarked Skipjack.

Mr Grimble's new, sweet voice oozed through the loudspeakers like liquid honey: 'My dear passengers, it gives me great pleasure to announce that the next stop will be the High Street. Take care stepping off the bus and I hope you all have a wonderful day.'

'Great – I'm hungry,' said Skipjack, leaping up.

The boys jumped off the bus and Skipjack led the way towards a red-and-white café with a big sign above the window which said, 'Mrs Happy's Pizzas'. As he pushed open the door, a large, orange-haired woman behind the counter looked up.

'Hiya, Oli! Hiya, Skip!' she cried when she saw the boys. 'This is smashing! Who's your friend?'

'His name's Ringo,' said Oli. 'You'll never guess where he's from.'

'Outer space? Ha-ha!' Sid gave Ringo a friendly bash on the back which made him lurch forwards with a splutter and clutch the counter for support.

Oli shook his head. 'Wrong. He's from Kalamistan!'

'Kalamistan!' Sid nearly clapped Ringo on the back again, but saw just in time that he had not yet recovered from the first assault. Instead she said, 'That's smashing! How is the old place? This calls for some extra-special pizza. Grab a stool, boys. I'll be right back.'

Ringo looked worried as he hoisted himself on to his stool. 'You didn't tell me she knew Kalamistan,' he whispered.

'Forgot,' shrugged Skipjack. 'Hey, Oli, what do you think will be on top of the extra-special pizza?'

'Twice as much as on an ordinary pizza, I hope,' replied Oli breezily. But guilt was pricking him all over with a very sharp pin.

Sid returned with three plates laden with squidgy slices of pizza. 'Extra-special pizza,' she announced, 'which is basically pizza with more pizza on top.'

'For extra-specially hungry customers,' added Skipjack and took a big bite.

Sid pulled up a stool and beamed at Ringo. 'So, Ringo, whereabouts in Kalamistan are you from?'

Ringo had been examining his pizza with great interest and was now lifting the first wedge off his plate with both hands. He hesitated. 'The middle,' he said and took a nibble.

'Oh, near Oblaski.'

'That's right,' mumbled Ringo.

'I was there, during the revolution,' said Sid. 'Chopped-off heads on railings – very messy. I suppose it's all calmed down now?'

'Mmmm,' said Ringo.

Sid frowned into the middle distance. 'What was the name of that castle on the river? Yuznush, wasn't it?'

Ringo's mouth was now so full of pizza he could only manage a nod.

'How well I remember days on that river,' sighed Sid and she continued to talk fondly about Oblaski and Yuznush while the boys ate their pizza. Finally Ringo pushed back his plate with a contented sigh.

'That was awesome,' he said happily.

'They just get better and better,' added Skipjack.

'Or else you boys get hungrier and hungrier,' chuckled Sid.

'Look, Ringo,' said Oli, pointing to the window. 'There's your mum.' Mrs Kuznet was peering in, one hand shading her eyes to cut out the reflection. When she saw Ringo she beckoned.

He flushed. 'She worries,' he said again. 'I'd better go.' He picked up his jacket, thanked Sid and departed.

It was not until after Ringo had gone that Oli noticed something black and shiny on the seat where his jacket had lain.

'It's his mobile,' he said, picking it up.

'He was right about always losing it,' grinned Skipjack.

Oli said, 'It's lucky I live so close. I can return it.' While he was examining the mobile he asked, 'So, Sid, what do you think of our new friend?'

'Smashing,' said Sid, piling up their empty plates, 'but he's not from Kalamistan.'

Oli looked up. 'How d'you know?'

'That castle I asked him about? It's not called Yuznush, it's called Bashkov. Yuznush is up in the mountains, a hundred miles away from the city.'

Skipjack shrugged. 'Yuznush, Bashkov, same difference. These Kalamistanis need to invent proper names for their castles. Then people wouldn't muddle them up.'

But Oli asked, 'Did you suspect all along he was lying?'

She shrugged. 'When you've been around as much as I have, you get a nose for these things. The question is: why would he lie about it?'

Why, indeed? thought Oli.

The boys parted at the Pond Lane bus stop and Oli headed towards Ringo's house to return the mobile. But as he walked up the path, he heard angry voices through an open window: Ringo and his mum were having an argument. Oli stopped to listen.

'I just think you are too friendly with those boys,' Mrs Kuznet was saying. 'You will give yourself away. We must be so careful until we can find our contact.'

'I am being careful,' Ringo told her. 'Oli and Skipjack don't suspect anything.'

'How can you be so sure?'

'Because they're really nice to me,' replied Ringo. Outside the window, Oli blushed.

'But you don't even know them!' his mother

cried. 'Soon you will think they are so nice that you can trust them with all our secrets and then you will tell them everything!'

'I wish I *could* tell them everything!' shouted Ringo. 'I hate having secrets!'

A door slammed: the conversation was over. Mystified, Oli crept away.

At home he found Tara sitting in the middle of the lawn beside a plate of silvery-brown mush and calling, 'Here, Kitty-Kitty!' through a tightly pinched nose.

'Have you seen a cat?' she called when she saw him.

'Loads,' he replied.

Tara's tongue made a sharp sound dangerously like the cocking of an AK-47 rifle. 'I didn't mean in your whole life,' she snapped. 'I meant just now. There's a stray cat around somewhere and I want it to be mine. I'm luring it with sardines. Sardines smell horrible.'

'No pain, no gain,' Oli told her.

He left her luring and went inside. Upstairs in his bedroom he closed the door and placed a chair against it and, having taken these anti-Tara precautions, sat down for a proper look at Ringo's mobile.

It was unlike any mobile he had ever seen: there were no buttons and no numbers and at first he couldn't even work out how to switch it on. Then his fingers felt two rubbery pads along the sides and he pressed them. The screen lit up. Oli watched, hoping to see familiar icons, but all that appeared were blobs: a yellow blob and two pale-blue blobs. Oli touched the white screen all over with his fingertip to see if anything else would appear but nothing did. He frowned. What did these apparently random blobs signify? He had no idea.

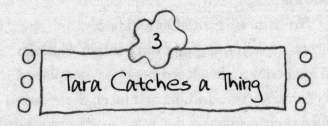

3
Tara Catches a Thing

'I've got a new pet,' Tara announced at supper that night.

'Eight legs, four legs, or no legs?' enquired Mum. Tara kept a whole collection of pets, ranging from cold-blooded to warm-blooded to green-blooded and from slimy to furry to exo-skeletal. They lived in cages and jars in the tree house, but tensions arose now and then when she let them out for exercise and Oli, who for some reason could not tell the difference between a woodlouse belonging to Tara and a nameless, unadopted woodlouse, trod on them.

'Three legs, actually,' said Tara. 'It's that stray cat. He couldn't resist the sardines so now he's in the tree house and he's mine.'

'Are you sure he's really a stray?' asked her mother.

'He must be. I know all the neighbours' cats and I've never seen this one before. Besides, he's really scrawny and he's only got three legs. He's very sweet, though. I'm going to call him Tripod.'

'Is he black and white, by any chance?' asked Oli.

Tara was instantly wary. 'He might be,' she said. 'Why?'

'He isn't a stray, you idiot. He belongs to the Kuznets. I've seen him in their house.'

'That doesn't mean he's theirs,' said Tara stubbornly.

'He's called Cuddles.'

'What an embarrassing name. Poor Tripod. Anyway, they obviously don't feed him enough, so they don't deserve to keep him.'

'That's hardly for you to decide,' said her mother. 'You'll have to let him go.'

Tara said nothing but she stuck her chin out in a sign that Oli knew well. So after supper he marched her to the tree house himself, to ensure the release of Cuddles. He waited below while she climbed the rope ladder, pushed open the trapdoor and disappeared inside.

A second later there was a terrible scream. Oli's blood turned to ice and he scrambled up the ladder, dreading the horrors he would find at the top.

Tara was pressed against the nearest wall, breathing heavily. In the opposite corner, baring fangs, was a Thing.

It was the size of a fox but that was the limit of its similarity to anything Oli had ever seen before. Bright orange and speckled with purple spots, it had big googly eyes and a snout like a warthog. Its head was topped with an explosion of wild orange hair, which spread to a mane and a ridge along its sloping back. It had a long forked tail and scaly feet with claws like sabres.

The three-legged cat was nowhere to be seen.

'That Thing has eaten Tripod!' wailed Tara.

Oli wondered whether it ate people as well as cats – it seemed to be eyeing them hungrily, dribbling green drool. He looked around for something he could use as a weapon but saw only a wooden chair.

'You get down the ladder,' he told his sister. 'I'll hold it off.'

Without taking her eyes off the Thing, Tara edged her way towards the trapdoor. Suddenly the Thing sprang forwards. Tara screamed and stumbled. Now she was on the floor, with the Thing about to land on her. Oli seized the chair.

But the Thing did not attack; it took a flying leap through the trapdoor and was gone.

And in the split-second
that it took to flash past him, Oli
noticed something strange: the Thing
had three legs.

He flung the chair aside, scrambled for
the rope ladder and slithered all the way
to the bottom, picking himself up just in
time to see the Thing scuttle through the
gate. Oli legged it across the garden and
out into the road. There was the Thing,
shooting along Pond Lane. As Oli caught
up, it leapt over the Kuznets' garden
fence and disappeared round the side
of the house.

Oli walked home thoughtfully.

He didn't know a lot about the wildlife
of Kalamistan, but he was pretty sure it
wouldn't contain anything quite like the
Thing.

He arrived back to find Tara in the
kitchen, describing the creature to Mum.

'It was purple and orange with massive
teeth and googly eyes and it was slobbering
green drool!'

Fortunately Tara had a habit of
exaggerating, so there was little danger of
Mum believing her.

'Are you sure that's what you saw?' she
asked.

Tara nodded emphatically. 'Positive! Ask Oli. Go on, Oli – tell her.' She faced him, arms crossed, chin in the air.

Oli looked vague. 'I suppose she's right about the googly eyes. I didn't notice any green drool. It was like some kind of big, hairy lizardy thing. I think I've seen it in the pet shop.'

'You have *not* seen it in the pet shop!' shouted Tara. 'And what kind of hairy lizardy thing eats a whole *cat*?'

'Are you sure the cat didn't just jump out of the window?' asked Mum.

'Positive, cos the window wasn't open. There was no way the cat could have got out.'

'In that case,' asked Mum, 'how did the hairy lizardy thing get in?'

Tara couldn't answer this so instead she glared at her brother and said, 'Anyway, I'm going to find out what it was.'

But although she spent an hour consulting all her animal books and the whole of the World Wide Web, she failed to identify anything that matched her memory of the Thing. This made her crosser than ever, and when she was finally dragged away from the computer and up to bed by Mum, she stuck her head round Oli's door.

'I know you know something about that Thing,' she hissed, 'and when I find out what it is, you'll be sorry you lied to Mum about it. So there.'

The next day was Sunday, which, for Oli and Skipjack, meant rugby at their local club. On this particular Sunday there was a tournament, which meant lots and lots of rugby, and so it wasn't until late in the afternoon that Oli was finally able to go round to Ringo's house with the mobile phone.

But Ringo wasn't at home. 'He has gone to visit Skipjack,' Mr Kuznet explained.

Trying to convince himself that he didn't mind at all, Oli set off for his best friend's house. But he decided not to tell Skipjack about the Thing; Skipjack would think owning a big, hairy-lizardy cat-eating creature was immensely cool, and Skipjack already thought Ringo was quite cool enough. As Oli approached the house he heard their voices from the back garden. 'No,

Ringo,' Skipjack was saying, 'in rugby you can *run* forwards but you have to throw the ball *backwards*. No, it isn't crazy – it makes complete sense. Hi, Oli! I'm teaching Ringo a proper game. You're just in time to help me show him a scrum.'

Oli didn't want Ringo to be able to play rugby, but he didn't want to be left out, either. So he said, 'OK. By the way, Ringo, you left this at Sid's,' and he held out the mobile phone.

Ringo was delighted. 'Oh, thanks, Oli.'

'It's an interesting mobile,' remarked Oli. 'Very unusual.'

Ringo looked uneasy. 'You . . . you didn't switch it on, did you?' he asked.

'I might have done,' replied Oli vaguely, 'just accidentally.'

Skipjack was bored of this conversation. 'Come on, let's do some more practice. You should see Ringo's passing, Oli. He's great.'

'Ringo seems to be great at everything,' said Oli.

Skipjack couldn't recognise a waspish remark if it stung him on the nose, but Ringo did. He

shot a quick
glance at Oli
and then looked
at the screen of his
mobile. From where Oli
stood he could see more blobs; a
green one and a blue one this time.
What did they mean? They meant
something to Ringo, who glanced up
at Oli, frowning. Oli quickly looked away.

'I should go,' said Ringo.

'I'll just show you how to kick,' said
Skipjack. 'Then you can take the ball
home and practise. Look, this is called a
kicking tee. You put it on the ground and
you put the ball in it like a boiled egg.
See? Then you kick it. Like this.'

Skipjack took a run-up and
booted the ball high into the air. It
landed in a tree.

'Was that
supposed to
happen?' asked
Ringo.

'Not exactly,' admitted Skipjack. 'I'll get a stick.'

He tootled off. In the awkward silence that now hung over Ringo and Oli, a nearby church clock began to chime six. Looking more and more worried, Ringo consulted his mobile yet again. A new blob had appeared, a yellow one, tiny but very bright. Ringo frowned for a moment, as if working out the significance of the blob, and then he drew in his breath sharply.

'I must go,' he muttered. 'I have to get home.' He started walking quickly over the grass.

'Stop!' shouted Oli. 'I want to ask you some questions!' Ringo broke into a run and Oli, without stopping to think, raced after him, dived at his legs and brought him to the ground.

'Great tackle!' called Skipjack, returning with his stick.

'Let me go!' cried Ringo.

'Not until you tell us who you really are,' demanded Oli, shaking him. 'Because you're not from Kalamistan and your cat isn't really a cat and that isn't a mobile phone you keep looking at. So who are you?'

Skipjack, drawing nearer, realised that this was no ordinary rugby tackle. 'Oli? What are you doing?'

'Ringo's been lying to us,' Oli replied, 'and I want to know why.'

'I can't tell you,' said Ringo, wriggling hard.

'Can't, or won't?'

'Can't,' insisted Ringo. 'You don't understand – it would put my whole family in danger. Let me go – I must get home.'

Oli stopped shaking Ringo and peered at his face. It was turning green. He quickly rolled away to the side; if Ringo was going to be sick, he wanted to be safely out of the firing line. He was seized with regret.

'I'm sorry, Ringo,' he muttered as he stood up. 'Are you OK?'

He held out a hand to help Ringo stand, but received no reaction. Ringo tried to stagger to his feet but he lurched forwards on to the grass again and then, as the others watched in horror, his whole body began to change. His neck seemed to stretch and there was a ripping

sound from his
T-shirt as a second
pair of arms
began to sprout,
which grew longer
and longer while
his legs became
shorter. His skin
turned bright
green and his face
transformed into
something utterly
unrecognisable.

Ringo had
turned into an
alien.

4
Ringo's Surprise

For several seconds nobody moved. Then the alien Ringo made a kind of gargling noise in his throat and fled to the nearest clump of bushes.

Oli and Skipjack turned to one another in stunned amazement.

'He's an alien,' Oli whispered.

'A green one,' Skipjack whispered back.

'With four arms,' whispered Oli.

'And ears like Dobby the House Elf, and *antennae*!' squeaked Skipjack.

As that seemed to cover everything, they stopped whispering and began to think.

Skipjack thought about all the aliens he had ever seen in films and added up the ones who did *not* have plans to blow up the Earth or exterminate the human race. Very few.

Oli thought about Ringo, hiding from them in

the bushes.

'Poor Ringo,' he said. 'We must help him.'

'Help him?' squeaked Skipjack. 'Are you crazy? How do we know he won't zap us with his laser gun? Or even worse, abduct us? I saw this film once—'

Oli interrupted him. 'Firstly he hasn't got a laser gun and secondly if he had wanted to zap us or abduct us he could have done it loads of times already, and thirdly he's our Friend.'

He took a step towards the bush. 'Ringo?' he called in a low voice.

Silence. Then a very soft gargle.

'We want to help you.'

Gargle-gargle.

'Skipjack's going to find a big blanket so that we can cover you up and take you back to your house. OK?'

Gargle-gargle.

'I'm guessing here that your mum and dad know you're an alien?'

Gargle-gargle.

It was a bit of a one-sided conversation which was not getting anywhere fast and Oli wondered whether the alien Ringo even understood English. He sent Skipjack on his blanket mission and, while he waited, he thought about the extraordinary transformation they had just seen. Ringo had clearly known he was about to turn into an alien, which was why he had tried to run away, so he must do it regularly, like a werewolf. His parents were probably aliens as well. What were all they doing here?

Skipjack came scurrying across the grass with his arms full of blanket. 'Sorry,' he panted. 'It's tartan.'

'I don't think Ringo will mind,' replied Oli. 'Ringo? Are you still there?'

Rustle-rustle. Gargle-gargle.

'Skipjack's got the blanket. We'll hold it up, ready to cover you. You've got to come out now, Ringo.'

They stood close to the bushes with the blanket held up high. Peeping round the sides they saw a green head rise from the undergrowth as Ringo stepped out. His clothes were all torn and his trainers had come off altogether. They draped the blanket over him so that only his feet

and ankles showed and together they helped him forwards.

Ringo allowed himself to be guided homewards without resisting. Whether or not he understood what they said, he seemed to sense that they were trying to help him. As they steered the strange blanketed figure along the road Oli reflected how lucky it was that he and Skipjack had a bit of a reputation for messing about; anyone who happened to pass them now would not think it strange at all that they were in the company of an Unidentified Tartan Object.

Just then they did see someone. A man was hurrying towards them and as he drew near the boys realised who it was.

'Mr Kuznet,' said Oli.

There was a loud gargle from Ringo.

Mr Kuznet's face was a picture of agitation as he spotted the green webbed feet sticking out from beneath the blanket. 'So it happened!' he exclaimed. 'We were so afraid that it would. Did anyone see?'

'Only us,' Oli replied. 'He hid in some bushes while we found something to cover him with.'

'Oh, thank you, thank you,' said Mr Kuznet as he took Ringo by the shoulders. The pair of them then had a long conversation which sounded like a couple of ostriches rinsing their tonsils. Oli walked ahead, checking that the way was clear, and Skipjack brought up the rear, enjoying Ringo's feet going *splat*, *splat*, *splat* on the pavement before him.

When they reached Pond Lane Mr Kuznet said to Oli and Skipjack, 'Will you come inside with us? We have many things to talk about.'

Skipjack looked doubtful: these were aliens, after all. Mr Kuznet noticed his reluctance. 'We will not zap you with our laser guns, Skipjack, or abduct you,' he assured him.

'Ah, but you might wipe our memories, so we forget all about you,' retorted Skipjack, who was an expert on alien tactics.

'I promise not to.'

'Or suck our brains out through our ears for experiments.'

'Absolutely not. Only Zolborgs do that.'

'Come on, Skip,' urged Oli.

'My wife has made pizza for supper,' said Mr Kuznet, 'as a treat for Ringo.'

(A cheerful gargle came from under the blanket.)

'I'm right behind you,' said Skipjack.

When Mrs Kuznet realised what had happened to her son she collapsed onto a chair and buried her head in her arms. 'Oh, Mr Kuznet, we are lost!' she wailed.

'Hush, Mrs Kuznet,' said her husband. 'Oli and Skipjack are friends. They helped our Ringo to stay safe. We owe them our thanks.'

He opened a cupboard and took out a bottle of blue medicine and a small measuring spoon.

'He takes a potion, you see, to keep him looking human,' he explained to Oli and Skipjack as he opened the bottle. 'We all do, but children can't take as much as adults, so the

effects wear off more quickly. Evening is always a
dangerous time.'

He poured a measure into the spoon and
tipped it into Ringo's mouth. Ringo swallowed
it and shuddered. Skipjack felt for him; he hated
taking medicine, too. Then he and Oli watched,
fascinated, as Ringo slowly turned human again.

They were dismayed to see how embarrassed he was.

'Welcome back, Ringo,' said Oli quickly. 'That was some trick.'

'Awesome,' nodded Skipjack. 'Just imagine what Doctor Levity would give you for that – half his shop, I should think.'

Ringo looked relieved. 'I must have given you a shock,' he said, but Oli shook his head.

'It's all my fault. If I hadn't pinned you down like that you would have been able to get away. I'm sorry.'

'I can see why you were angry,' Ringo said. 'I hate it when people keep secrets from me.' He took his mobile from the pocket of his now very tattered trousers and held it out. 'This is a Hostility Detector,' he explained. 'It shows you how people within a fifty-metre radius feel about you, so that you are warned if someone is hostile. See? These two green blobs are you two. Green means friendly. The yellow blobs are my parents. Yellow is family love. Earlier your blob was blue, Oli. Blue is hostility. But I'm not surprised you didn't trust me. I'm not very good at pretending to be normal.'

'Skipjack here has the same problem,' Oli told him. 'Can I have a go?' Ringo handed him the Hostility Detector and Oli pressed the pads along the edge. Four green blobs appeared on the screen. Oli looked pleased.

'Let me try,' begged Skipjack. Ringo showed him how to hold it and Skipjack beamed round when he saw the four green blobs. Then he had a thought: 'Hey, Ringo, can this machine tell if a girl fancies you?'

Ringo grinned. 'It sure can. That would be a pink blob. If you ever want to check someone out I can lend it to you.'

'Do you all carry one of these?' asked Oli.

Mr Kuznet shook his head. 'No, usually only children, because children have not yet learnt to use their instinct the way adults can. The Hostility Detector helps a child to develop this instinct and it will also detect an enemy in time for you to take action.'

'This must be the most useful gizmo ever invented,' said Skipjack, thinking of all the enemies he would be able to avoid if he could see their blue blobs coming from fifty metres away.

'But where are you all from?' asked Oli. 'Why are you here?'

'It is a long story,' replied Mr Kuznet. 'I will tell you everything.' And this is what he said.

'We come from the planet Quorkidellian, far away in the Outer Spondeeling Galaxy. Ours is a peaceful planet, a beautiful planet. It is like Earth – blue and green. We are very fond of Earth. We have been visiting for thousands of years, doing research and watching you develop. We even helped the ancient Earthoids to construct buildings – like the pyramids – and we tried to teach them about the universe, but they started

to believe we were Gods, so we had to leave. We still visit often, but secretly now, taking the form of Earthoids so as not to draw attention to ourselves. There may be many of us here at any time, living undetected among you just like we ourselves were until Ringo's little accident. Some Earthoids, specially selected ones, have become contacts for us. They gather information and help us when we visit. It was such a contact who sent us a message three days ago, while we were orbiting in search of somewhere to land. That is why we came here, to this town. We were so excited to receive the message because it meant we would find a friendly face here, but I have been trying ever since to reach this contact again and I have had no response at all.'

Oli asked, 'Are you positive the message was from your contact?'

'Positive,' nodded Mr Kuznet.

'I wonder who could have sent it.'

'Come on, Oli,' put in Skipjack. 'There's any amount of nutters in this town who could be trying to make contact with aliens.'

'When did you receive the message?' asked Oli.

'At three o'clock on Thursday,' replied Mr Kuznet. 'I noted it in the ship's log.'

Skipjack sat up. 'Three o'clock on Thursday? Er, what did the message say?'

'"Hoombinny-squilpok",' replied Mr Kuznet. 'It's a pre-arranged signal. So you see, only a Specially Selected Earthoid could have sent such a message.'

'But, that was me!' squeaked Skipjack. 'I sent that message!'

Mr Kuznet stared at him in surprise. 'Are *you* a Specially Selected Earthoid?' he asked doubtfully.

'I don't *think* so,' said Skipjack.

'Then, how did you know the code?' asked Ringo.

'It's one of Doctor Levity's magic words,' Skipjack explained. 'He says everyone's fed up of "Abracadabra", so he says "Hoombinny-squilpok" instead. I always thought he had just made it up.'

'Well, there's the answer,' said Oli with a grin. 'Your Earthoid Contact is none other than Doctor Levity.'

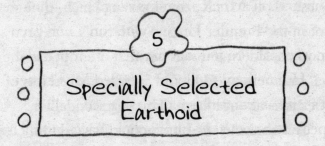

5

Specially Selected Earthoid

Once Oli and Skipjack had explained who
Doctor Levity was, and Ringo had added his
own high praise of a man who handed out
free boomerangs in return for ear-waggles, the
Kuznets looked very pleased and wanted to meet
him without delay. Oli suggested inviting him to
their house for, as he put it, 'a nice surprise'.

'Anyway, Doctor Levity's got a car – well, a
camper-van actually,' he explained, 'whereas
you'd have to take the bus to get to the joke shop,
which on a Sunday evening would mean waiting
for ages. Also Skipjack and I wouldn't be able to
come and we really want to know what happens.'

So Oli telephoned Doctor Levity and then
he and Skipjack rang their parents to ask if they
could stay at the Kuznets' for a bit longer. While

they waited for Doctor Levity to arrive they polished off Mrs Kuznet's pizza (which, though not in the Premier League with Sid's, was pretty good considering it was her first attempt *and* she was an alien) and Oli and Skipjack asked lots of questions about life on planet Quorkidellian.

'Tell us about the blue potion,' asked Oli. 'How does it work?'

'Over all the years that Quorkidellians from our planet have been coming here,' explained Mr Kuznet, 'we have been taking microscopic cell samples from Earthoids to study. The cells from an individual Earthoid can be mixed with other ingredients to create a potion which makes whoever drinks it look exactly like that particular Earthoid. Samples are stored in a special place and some of them have corresponding documents – identity cards and so on – for use on visits to Earth. My own appearance is taken from a real person called Mr Kuznet from Kalamistan and I have an exact copy of his passport in case I have to prove who I am.'

'And Ringo? And Mrs Kuznet?'

'Unfortunately we left in such a hurry that

there was not time to make potions for Ringo and my wife that would give us all a good family resemblance. I could only select a ready-made one for Ringo that I knew was from a boy of the right age. The range for women of Mrs Kuznet's age was very small. Mrs Kuznet wanted to use a sample that was taken about twenty years ago from Queen Elizabeth II but I didn't think that was wise.'

Mrs Kuznet shook her head. 'It was very mean of you not to allow it, Mr Kuznet. You spoiled my one chance to look like royalty. And now I am a Bulgarian washerwoman.'

Mr Kuznet said, 'I am sorry, my dear,' but added hurriedly, 'Anyway, I think you look very nice.'

There was a sound at the back door and the Kuznets' skinny three-legged cat slunk in through the flap.

Mrs Kuznet said, 'You'd better block up the cat-flap for tonight, Mr Kuznet. He'll be changing soon and we don't want him seen.'

'So what's Cuddles really, then?' enquired Oli.

'He's a fork-tailed Spogmondish Drongbat,' said Ringo.

Oli decided privately to stick with 'Thing'.

There was a knock on the door. Oli and Skipjack both ran to open it.

'Oh good,' said Doctor Levity when he saw them. 'Then I am at the right house.'

'Did you bring Daisy?' asked Skipjack, who was keen to see if she would be a pink blob.

'No, I left her with Sid. What's all this about?'

'You'd never believe us if we told you,' said Oli, 'so you'd better come and see for yourself.'

Pleasantly intrigued, Doctor Levity followed the boys through the hall to the kitchen, where the first person he saw was Ringo.

'Hello again,' he said. 'How's the boomerang?' Then he saw Mr and Mrs Kuznet. 'You must be Ringo's parents.'

'That is right.' Mr Kuznet rose from his chair and welcomed Doctor Levity warmly, clasping his hand and shaking it with vigour. 'Thank you for coming. You must be wondering why we have invited you here. I will give you a clue: Hoombinny-squilpok.' His dark-brown eyes glowed with mischievous humour.

Doctor Levity repeated slowly, '"Hoombinny-squilpok"?'

'Yabbaflibba-boing!' replied Mr Kuznet with a chuckle.

Doctor Levity's eyebrows shot up. 'You're not from Quorkidellian?' he exclaimed. 'This is fantastic! I should have guessed when I met Ringo in the shop – no Earthoid boy could waggle his ears like that. But what are those two doing here?' He waved an arm at Oli and Skipjack. 'Don't say you're planning to use them for experiments. You'll get some very bizarre results.'

'Hush! Do not mention experiments,' Mr Kuznet told him, 'or Skipjack will run away. No, no. These boys have been excellent friends to our Ringo. Now, please sit down and I will explain why we are here. Not long ago, our people elected a new Prime Minister, a Zolborg called Naphax. Some of us in government had suspected for a long time that he was not to be trusted, but he was elected nevertheless by the usual method of promising everything to everyone. So now he is the most powerful man on the planet.'

Skipjack frowned. 'Isn't a Zolborg one of the ones who suck brains out through ears?'

Mr Kuznet nodded.

'Does he do it with a straw?' asked Oli.

'Sometimes, I believe.'

'I'm glad our Prime Minister doesn't do that,' remarked Skipjack.

'You are lucky,' Mr Kuznet agreed. 'Now I

should explain that we have a special mineral on our planet called promethium. Promethium is an important source of power and it is also used for weapons. All the promethium that we mine is stored under high security and it is my job, as Promethium Protector, to guard it. We are a peaceful people and our weapons are only used to defend us against hostile aliens. However, I recently made a terrible discovery: Zolborg Naphax is planning to invade our neighbouring planet of Blix Formenta 5. And if he is successful I know his campaign will not end there; it would not be enough for a Zolborg like Naphax to be the ruler of one planet or even two – he will want to rule an entire empire. In order to build enough extra weapons to do this he needs access to the promethium stores. Of course, I refused to give him the key. Then I heard that he was sending his soldiers to capture my family and hold them in the prison he has built in the Black Wastes, a terrible place where the guards are armed with Dream-Readers and torment you with your worst nightmares. I needed to get my family to safety and time was running out, so

we took the only course possible: we escaped
in a spaceship. We had just reached your solar
system when we learnt that Zolborg Naphax
was chasing us. So we abandoned ship and came
down to Earth in a satellite pod. The rest you
know.'

'And Zolborg Naphax?' asked Doctor Levity.
'Where is he now?'

'He continued to follow our ship,' replied Mr
Kuznet, 'but he will catch up with it soon and
realise that we have tricked him. It won't take
him long to guess where we must have bailed
out.'

'Do you think he'll follow you here?' asked
Skipjack, who had decided that Zolborg Naphax
was exactly the sort of alien he didn't want to
meet.

Mr Kuznet shrugged. 'It would be difficult for him to track us down – we could be anywhere on Earth. He would be looking out for signals. And that brings us to another problem: if we are to be rescued we need to send messages to our allies, but the more messages we send, the more likely Zolborg Naphax is to intercept them and discover our location.'

'Can't you escape in your pod?' asked Skipjack.

Mr Kuznet shook his head. 'It was badly damaged when we landed.'

'Perhaps we could mend it,' suggested Oli.

'I am afraid it's beyond repair,' said Mr Kuznet. 'And even if we could mend it, our little pod has no Cosmic Overdrive and without that we would take thousands of years to reach home.

We need a proper ship.'

'Where is your pod?' asked Skipjack, thinking how cool it would be to see a real UFO.

'On the heath outside the town,' said Mr Kuznet. 'After we crashed we removed everything we could and hid the rest under piles of branches.'

'Do your allies know that you came to this galaxy when you escaped?' asked Doctor Levity.

Mr Kuznet shook his head. 'There wasn't time to tell anyone and I did not dare send a message.'

Doctor Levity frowned. 'What are the chances of a friendly ship coming within messaging distance now?'

'Very small,' Mr Kuznet told him. 'Your planet is on an outer spiral arm on the quietest side of the galaxy. There isn't much passing traffic.'

'Well, if the chance of messages being picked up by a friend is very small and the chance of messages being picked up by Zolborg Naphax is quite large,' sighed Doctor Levity, 'you'd better just sit tight for a while.'

Oli and Skipjack both got a lift home in the

camper-van.

'How did you get to be a Specially Selected Earthoid anyway?' asked Skipjack.

But Doctor Levity would say no more than, 'I think it must have been magic, pure magic.'

It was past nine o'clock when Oli arrived home and he was surprised to see that the tree-house light was still on. He went to the foot of the rope ladder and called, 'Tara?'

'Shh!'

'What are you doing up there?'

'Catching the Thing,' hissed Tara. 'But it won't come while you're there. Go away.'

Oli was about to tell his sister that the Thing was not hers to catch because it belonged to the Kuznets when he realised just how careless this would have been. He shuddered to think how much Silence Money she would have extracted from him in return for keeping that secret. For Tara was saving up to run away to Timbuktu, and her favourite source of funds was the Bank of Oli.

He turned to go and stumbled over a big metal bucket. A terrific clatter echoed through the silent night, like a dozen armoured knights doing star jumps. A furious head poked out of the tree-house window.

'Shut up! You're ruining *everything*!' hissed Tara.

'You shouldn't leave buckets standing about in the dark for people to fall over,' muttered Oli.

'How else am I going to catch the Thing?' she demanded. 'Put it back. And don't forget the bait.'

The bait turned out to be leftover pasta with meatballs and was by now strewn all over the grass. Oli picked up one meatball, dropped it into the bucket and left Tara the Thing-Hunter well alone.

When he came down to breakfast the next morning his sister was already at the table.

'Did you catch the Thing?' he asked.

'Of course I didn't. Not after you made all that noise falling over the bucket. But earlier on I saw Tripod again, which is strange because as we know the Thing ate him, so he should have been turned into Thing-poo by now. It just proves that cats really do have nine lives.'

'That would explain it,' agreed Oli.

'He wouldn't come near me, though,' sighed Tara. 'I probably remind him of being eaten.'

'I'm not sure you should be trying to catch this Thing at all,' said Mum. 'It's probably dangerous, and it must belong to someone. Exotic pets are very expensive.'

Tara brightened. 'In that case I can ask for a reward and the owner will pay me lots of money for returning it,' she said.

'You can't ask for money to return something when you've stolen it in the first place,' her mother told her. 'It isn't moral.'

Oli heard the sound of the newspaper being delivered through the letterbox, so he left his mum and Tara to discuss morality and wandered through to the hall to fetch it. As he was returning to the kitchen, he glanced casually at the headline and then stopped in his tracks. Shouting up at him from the front page were the big black words:

UFO FOUND ON HEATH!

Oli's heart sank. He skimmed through the article.

'I SAW LIGHTS!' CLAIMS LOCAL RESIDENT.

Debris from an Unidentified Flying Object has been found on No-man's Heath. Local inhabitant Grundy Thicket of Dingley Dell discovered the wreckage hidden under a pile of branches yesterday, after a two-day search. 'I saw lights over the heath on Thursday night,' explained Mr Thicket. 'I knew something strange had landed and I couldn't rest until I had found it.' Mr Thicket is now conducting tours of the area at £5.00 per person.

'Mum!' yelled Oli. 'I'm going to Ringo's house!'
'What about your breakfast?'
'I'll have something there. See you later.'

The Kuznets greeted Oli's news with dismay.

Their precious pod had represented the last link with home and its discovery put a definite end to any faint hopes they might still have had of using it to escape. In addition, as Mr Kuznet pointed out, people would now be on the lookout for anything – and anyone – connected with UFOs. Their presence in the town had just become a lot more risky.

'And to think that we were *seen*, Mr Kuznet,' cried Mrs Kuznet. 'How are we to know that this Thicket man wasn't watching us as we hid our pod? He may even have followed us here!'

'I promise you, Mrs Kuznet,' said Oli, 'that if Grundy Thicket knew you were here he'd be charging tourists a hundred pounds each to visit your house. My mum always says he'd sell his own granny if anyone paid him enough.'

But Mrs Kuznet was not to be comforted and she immediately banned Ringo from leaving the house.

Skipjack arrived, having heard the news as well, and Oli left him to cheer up the grounded Ringo with a rugby ball while he caught the bus into town to learn more.

He found the High Street in a whirlwind of
UFO excitement, with people rushing about
everywhere looking for aliens. Newly arrived
television crews were trying to find witnesses to
interview and busloads of curious visitors had
rolled up to join the fun. Oli popped into the
Pizza Café but Sid was busy inventing a Cosmic
Pizza to sell to the tourists and did not have time
for a chat.

He tried the joke shop next. Daisy was there,
blowing bubble gum and counting sets of

vampire teeth.

'Grandpa's on the roof,' she told him.

This seemed as likely a place as any to find
Doctor Levity so Oli set off up the narrow
winding stairs that led all the way through the
tall thin house to a small wooden door at the
very top. Oli knew from occasions when he and
Skipjack had helped to exercise Doctor Levity's
white doves that this door opened out on to a
small flat roof between the pointed gables. Here
indeed was Doctor Levity, setting up a telescope.

'How are our friends the Kuznets?' he enquired.

'Worried,' replied Oli.

'As well they might be.' Doctor Levity finished tightening the final bolt on the tripod and straightened up. 'If their friend Zolborg Naphax is anywhere about, all this fuss is bound to attract his attention.'

'Is that what this telescope is for?' asked Oli. 'Are you going to look out for him?'

Doctor Levity shrugged his shoulders in a gesture of untypical helplessness. 'It's about all I can do, Oli.' He gazed up at the blue sky. 'We know so little about what goes on out there. Some day we will find whole worlds, just like ours. Boys like you, old men like me. We must hope that the ones who find us first are more like the Kuznets and less like Zolborg Naphax.'

Oli left him with his telescope and returned to Pond Lane. He did not mention Doctor Levity's fears to the Kuznets, who already seemed anxious enough, and when Ringo begged him and Skipjack to stay for supper they agreed and tried very hard to make the family laugh with stories about their own scary encounters with the likes of Mr Grimble and Slugger Stubbins. Mrs Kuznet had cooked a kind of stew which was strange but not bad and when Oli asked what was in it she said, 'drogaboo stock', which didn't really answer his question.

'What I like about your meals, Mrs Kuznet,' said Skipjack, 'is that you don't bother with the boring stuff like cabbage and sprouts.'

'That's because green food is like poison to us,' explained Ringo, 'and we aren't allowed to eat any.'

Skipjack sighed. 'I wish I was an alien,' he said.

6
UFO Investigation Unit

Next morning's newspaper came earlier than usual so by the time Oli came downstairs Tara was already poring over the front page. Oli read the headline over her shoulder:

MORE LIGHTS!
SPACE EXPERT TO
INVESTIGATE

Local resident Grundy Thicket says he saw more bright lights above No-man's Heath last night. 'These lights were like laser beams,' he said. 'They were definitely from another UFO.' Mr Thicket is now conducting tours of the area at £10.00 per person.

Meanwhile Government Expert

Colonel T. Carbide will arrive today from The National Space Centre to investigate the site and identify the debris.

'Grundy Thicket is such a greedy cheat,' complained Tara. 'He's obviously inventing all these UFOs just to get rich.'

'Perhaps he wants to run away to Africa too,' remarked Oli. 'You could go together.'

Disappointingly, Tara wasn't even listening. 'I know what I'll do,' she said, her eyes gleaming with Plot. 'I'll tell the newspapers that I've seen a UFO in our garden. Then I can charge people £10 to come here and I'll make as much money as Grundy Thicket.'

But her mum soon put an end to these dreams of fabulous wealth. 'I am not,' she said firmly, 'having hoards of tourists trampling all over my flower beds. You'll just have to find another way to get to Timbuktu.'

Oli went round to Ringo's house after breakfast and was surprised to find all the curtains tightly drawn. Perhaps the Kuznets were still asleep? He went round to the back and knocked softly on the kitchen door. After much scuffling and urgent whispering, the nearest curtain tweaked and through a tiny crack peeked a wary eye that Oli recognised as Mr Kuznet's. A moment later the lock turned and the door was opened.

A hand reached out, gripped Oli by the arm and yanked him into the house. This had been done to Oli once before, but only by Skipjack, when Slugger Stubbins was laying siege. To be greeted this way by the normally charming Mr Kuznet was surprising. So, as Oli picked himself up off the floor and heard the door being re-locked, he was surprised.

'Laser beams in the sky last night,' whispered Mr Kuznet by way of explanation. 'They came down on the heath! Zolborg Naphax has landed!'

'Oh, I wouldn't worry too much about those,' Oli told him. 'Tara says Grundy Thicket didn't really see any lights at all – he just made them up to earn even more money from the tourists.'

'You don't understand,' said Ringo. '*We* saw the lights, from this house. Dad and I have been taking turns to watch the sky and last night there were laser beams. And then Doctor Levity rang to say that he had seen them, too.'

'Oh, Mr Kuznet!' wailed Mrs Kuznet. 'It is Zolborg Naphax – he is sure to find us! Any minute now, he will come crashing through that door and demand the key to the promethium store and if you do not give it to him, Mr Kuznet, we will all be exterminated!'

She had hardly finished speaking when there was a loud bang on the door. All three Kuznets and Oli jumped two feet in the air and looked at one another in alarm.

'Hello?' called a voice. 'Earth calling Ringo?'

'Skipjack!' exclaimed Oli. He ran to open the door.

Skipjack took one look at the circle of gloomy faces and gulped. 'It's the brain-sucker, isn't it?' he said.

Ringo nodded and told him about the lights.

Oli felt a strong urge to take action. 'I think we should go into town and see if we can find any sign of Zolborg Naphax,' he said.

Ringo asked his parents, 'Can I go with them?'

'Of course you can't go with them!' cried Mrs Kuznet. 'The very idea!'

'Why not?' argued Ringo. 'Zolborg Naphax wouldn't even recognise me – he'd just think I'm another Earthoid boy, like Oli and Skipjack.'

'On the other hand, you won't recognise him either,' said Mr Kuznet, 'because he will have taken the blue potion and he'll look like an Earthoid as well.'

'All the more reason for me to go along,' insisted Ringo. 'I could spot him with my

Hostility Detector.'

'You are not leaving this house and that's final,' declared Mrs Kuznet.

'Dad?' pleaded Ringo.

Mr Kuznet turned to his wife. 'We cannot keep him locked up here all day, Mrs Kuznet. And we've always taught him to face up to fears, not to hide away.'

Mrs Kuznet drew herself up to her full height, which was not very much, and glared at her husband. Oli never knew that a Bulgarian washerwoman could look so fierce. 'Ringo is not going into town and that is final,' she announced.

So that was that, and Oli and Skipjack set off alone. 'Let's go up to the heath first,' suggested Oli. 'We can see what's left of the Kuznets' pod and maybe talk to the Government Space Expert.'

A lane led up to No-man's Heath, widening at the top into a parking area which now swarmed with people: tourists, self-appointed guides (or locals out to make a quick quid), stall-holders selling souvenirs . . . even Sid was there with her Cosmic Pizza. But despite the hullabaloo

it was not hard to locate the Government Space Expert, for in the midst of the human sea, like a giant cuboid island, was a massive silver lorry. The sides of the lorry were printed with the words 'MOBILE UFO INVESTIGATION UNIT' and each corner of its roof sprouted dishes and antennae of all shapes and sizes, pointing in every direction.

Skipjack said in an awed voice, 'Just think of the sports channels you could get if you lived in that lorry.'

'Why are all those people gathered round it?' wondered Oli.

'Perhaps the Government Space Expert is going to sell ice creams,' suggested Skipjack hopefully.

They pushed through to the front of the crowd for a better view and found themselves in a scrimmage of other kids.

'What's everyone waiting for?' Oli asked the nearest boy.

'Colonel Carbide is going to make a statement,' he replied, 'about the UFO.'

'Looks like we're just in time,' murmured Oli to Skipjack as the lorry's rear doors began to open and a man emerged from the darkness within.

Colonel T. Carbide was two metres tall, heavily built and dressed in white anti-contamination overalls and rubber boots. He planted his feet in the doorway and pushed back the hood of his overalls, revealing a thick neck and a crew cut. His eyes were hidden by dark glasses and his nose was clearly the survivor of many a punch-up. In short, he looked the kind of man whose brain any sensible alien would think very seriously about before attempting to remove with a straw.

Colonel Carbide cleared his throat and the crowd fell obediently silent. Then he spoke, in a slow, deep voice. 'Greetings, all. I have completed my examination of the crash site and I can now confirm that the debris comes from a weather satellite and not, I repeat *not*, from an alien craft. You can all return home. There is nothing to see. Thank you.'

There was a disappointed murmur from the crowd. 'What about Grundy Thicket's laser beams?' someone shouted.

'Mr Thicket has decided that he was wrong about the laser beams,' answered Colonel Carbide. 'He was confused. He now thinks they were the eyes of his sheep reflected in the light of his torch.'

'What, thirty feet in the air?' countered the man. 'I didn't know Grundy's sheep were that big. Or is he breeding a flock that can fly?'

There was a ripple of laughter. Colonel Carbide removed his dark glasses and focused the man in his sights. 'Mr Thicket was confused,' he repeated.

The man swallowed and nodded.

'Aliens have not landed on No-man's Heath,' said Colonel Carbide.

The man nodded again.

'End of statement,' said Colonel Carbide. As the crowd, silent and disappointed now, began to disperse, the boy next to Oli called out, 'What's inside your lorry?'

'This vehicle is equipped with high-tech devices to detect and capture extra-terrestrials. It is one hundred per cent alien-proof,' Colonel Carbide told him.

'That's strange – back on my planet we have lorries that are a hundred per cent Earthoid-proof,' joked Skipjack.

Colonel Carbide looked at him sharply. 'That is not funny,' he announced and withdrew behind the doors of his truck.

Skipjack was pink and offended. 'I thought it was funny,' he said. 'Did you think it was funny, Oli?'

'Of course I did. And Daisy would have done, too. Colonel Carbide just doesn't have a sense of humour. What I want to know is why Grundy Thicket changed his story about the lights.'

'Let's go and ask him,' suggested Skipjack.

'Good idea,' agreed Oli and they set off.

7
Grundy Thicket

'Anyhow, I've always wanted to find out if the
rumours are true,' said Skipjack as they turned
off the lane onto the track that led to Dingley
Dell, Grundy Thicket's small farm on the edge
of the heath.

'What rumours?' asked Oli.

'About Grundy Thicket's granny. She
disappeared five years ago. I heard he sold her to
a travelling circus.'

As the boys approached the cottage, a bundle
of fur with a leg at each corner shot out of a
ramshackle shed and barked at them furiously
before seizing a mouthful of Skipjack's trouser
leg and giving him a good shake. One of the
cottage windows opened and a hand emerged.
The hand picked up a flowerpot from the sill
and lobbed it, flower and all, towards the canine

assailant. The flowerpot sailed through the air like Halley's Comet, leaving a crumbly tail of earth and landing inches from the dog's nose. With a yelp of outrage, the animal fled back to the safety of the sheds where no flowerpots flew, leaving the boys to advance on the cottage unmolested. They found the door open and when a voice from inside called, 'You won't be getting a red carpet, so you might as well just walk in,' they did, trying not to tread on any of the scrawny chickens that were pecking about in the hall.

They found the Thickets just finishing their lunch. As well as Mr and Mrs Thicket, there were several small Thickets who all looked as

scrawny and scruffy as the dog and the hens. Skipjack noticed to his satisfaction that there was no sign of a granny.

'What can I do for you, lads?' asked Grundy Thicket, tearing a ragged hunk of bread from the loaf to wipe around his plate.

'We came to ask you about the UFOs,' replied Oli.

'I see,' nodded Grundy Thicket. He popped the bread, brown and dripping, into his mouth and munched thoughtfully. Oli noticed that his nose twitched while he chewed which, together with his beady eyes and excessively whiskery sideburns, gave him the appearance of a giant rodent.

'Run along outside, kids,' said Mrs Thicket,

starting to clear the table. There was a cacophony of chair-leg scraping as the children raced one another out of the room. Mrs Thicket carried a pile of plates over to a sink that was already so full of pots and pans that there was hardly room for a teaspoon, so she dumped the plates on the floor, where a cat began to lick them.

Grundy Thicket leaned back and put his hands behind his head. 'I'm sorry to disappoint you, lads,' he said, 'but I've got nothing to say that I didn't already say to the colonel. The first lights must have come from that weather satellite and the second lights were a mistake.'

'But how can you mistake laser beams for sheep's eyes?' asked Oli.

Grundy Thicket shrugged. 'That's exactly what I've been asking myself and what all those good folk who bought tickets to see the site asked me, too, and all I can say is that it was an honest mistake. You'd be surprised at the gleam that a sheep can get in its eye when it's in the mood for mischief.' He stood up and stretched. 'Sorry, lads, but that's all I can tell you. Now, if you don't mind, I've got to be getting back to work.

No peace for the wicked, eh?' He gave a brief chortle, like the rasp of a rhino's bottom on a thorn tree, and sauntered out.

Left alone in the kitchen with the scavenging cat, Oli scratched his head while Skipjack took out his Misera Ball and began tossing it absentmindedly in the air.

'I don't believe he's really changed his mind,' remarked Oli. 'But why would he chuck away the chance to earn loads of dosh from his UFO Tours by saying the lights were really from his sheep, which also makes him look like a loony? I know Tara would never do it, and this is a man who would sell his own granny. In fact, according to you, he *has* sold his own granny. It just doesn't make sense.'

Oli suddenly became aware that they were being watched and he glanced towards the window. Five little pairs of eyes were peeping in and following the Misera Ball as it went up towards the ceiling and back down again, wailing all the way. The peepers gave Oli an idea and he leaned in close to Skipjack.

'Keep throwing,' he whispered. 'You'll see

why.' Then he said in a louder voice, 'Come on, Skip. Let's go.'

They picked their way through the chickens to the door and started back down the track that led from Dingley Dell to the lane. Skipjack continued to toss his Misera Ball in the air, while behind them darting shadows and the odd rustle hinted at unseen company.

'Hey, Oli,' said Skipjack. 'I think we're being followed.'

'I *know* we're being followed,' replied Oli, and when they had rounded a corner in the track and were hidden from the cottage he said in a loud voice,

'What a shame that Mr Thicket didn't see the second lot of lights after all. Especially when we were so keen to find out more information that you would have given him your Misera Ball, wouldn't you, Skip?'

'No, I wouldn't actually—' began Skipjack (sharp nudge from Oli) 'I mean, yes, I would. I would give my Misera Ball to *anyone* who could tell us *anything* about the lights.'

'We know about the lights!' squeaked a chorus

behind them.

They turned round to see a flock of Thicket children tumbling out of the hedgerows. Oli looked very surprised to find them there and once they had picked themselves up he asked, 'Do you *really* know about the lights?'

'Yes! Yes! Yes!' The Thickets were jumping up and down now, like fleas on a trampoline.

'That's fantastic,' said Oli. 'Why don't you tell us all about them?'

They all started talking at once in such a blizzard of words and waving arms that Oli and Skipjack couldn't understand anything. Oli put up his hand. 'It would be better if just one of you told us.'

The jumping started again. 'Me! Me! Me!' cried the children.

'It doesn't matter who,' said Oli patiently. 'Everyone can share the Misera Ball. What about you?' He pointed to the tallest Thicket, a boy of about six with a mop of red hair. The boy took a proud step forward and began to explain. It soon became clear that he was missing all his front teeth, but Oli and Skipjack got the gist of what

he was saying, which was as follows.

The children had not seen the first lights because they had been asleep, but the following day they had all gone out on the heath with their father to look for the thing he told them had landed and, after a lot of hunting, they had found the crashed remains under a pile of branches.

'And? Was it a weather satellite?' demanded Oli.

The boy didn't know – there was a lot of twisted metal and broken bits from computers and engines, but they had found one thing that couldn't have come from a satellite: a green, glowing bone, about as long as a pencil. When Oli asked what had happened to the bone, the boy said that Colonel Carbide had taken it.

'What about the second lights?' asked Oli. 'The ones like laser beams?'

They had all seen those, said the boy, because of Fleabag having her puppies that night and everyone being awake. The lights had come out of the sky quite slowly and hovered at about tree-top height. Then they had darted off to one side and hovered a bit more. Then they had moved further away and slowly come down to land. His dad had taken a pitchfork and run out on to the heath but by the time he had reached the spot where the lights had come down there was no sign of the UFO, just a circle of scorch marks on the grass.

'How big was the circle?' asked Oli.

'About thith big,' said the boy, holding both arms out at full stretch.

'Did Colonel Carbide see the circle?' asked Oli.

'Yeth,' said the boy. 'He thaid it wath lightning.'

Oli frowned. 'And what did he say the bone was?'

'A lucky charm,' said the boy. 'He thaid the men who make the weather thatelliteth alwayth put thomething in them for good luck.'

'Funny that he hasn't mentioned that to anyone else,' said Oli thoughtfully.

'He probably doesn't want people to know what a bunch of loonies are in charge of our weather satellites,' Skipjack pointed out. 'Green glowing bones, indeed.'

Oli asked the boy why his dad now denied having seen the laser beams. He replied that Colonel Carbide had ordered him to and warned that the whole family could otherwise be arrested for frightening people.

'Can you show us the first crash site?' asked Oli, but the boy shook his head. Anyone who was caught poking around it would be taken away in Colonel Carbide's lorry.

'Well, just tell us which direction it's in,' said Oli.

The boy pointed back up the track. 'Go all the way to the end. Look for the tall pine treeth. Can we have the ball now?'

'Yeah, sure. Skip?'

So Skipjack took one last look at his beloved Misera Ball and tossed it over to the boy, who caught it neatly. The other Thickets gathered round him eagerly and Oli and Skipjack were forgotten.

They retraced their steps back up the hill past the cottage, until the track grew fainter and fainter and became finally just more heath. With the help of the tall pine trees, the boys soon spotted the remains of the Kuznets' pod under a sheet of blue plastic. Colonel Carbide had cordoned it off with posts and tape and numerous signs telling them to Keep Out, but they ignored these, of course. Under the plastic was a sad heap of smashed and buckled metal, just as the Thicket boy had described.

'Poor Kuznets,' sighed Skipjack. 'They'd get further in a supermarket trolley than they would in their pod now.'

'It's a miracle they weren't hurt,' said Oli. 'Let's go and tell Doctor Levity what we've found out. He might have an idea about what we can do next.'

'And he might have another

Misera Ball,' said Skipjack. 'And he might let me have it for free.'

Doctor Levity did have another Misera Ball and, although he didn't let Skipjack have it for free, he let him have it on loan until his next Pocket Money Day. So Skipjack was happy again.

They told him all about their visit to the heath and what they had learned.

Doctor Levity nodded. 'What you have to remember is that, regardless of what Colonel Carbide found or what he privately thinks, he would never say publicly that the debris was from a UFO. Think of the panic. He would be under strict instructions from the Government to say it was something quite normal, like a weather satellite, and let all the fuss die down while he quietly went on examining it. Of course, it's always possible that he really thinks it is a weather satellite, but I doubt it. We have to hope that he finds Zolborg Naphax before Zolborg Naphax finds the Kuznets.'

Not very far away at all, Zolborg Naphax smiled

to himself as he stretched out in his hiding place to rest. It had been a busy day but everything was going well. To think that only forty-eight hours ago he had been cursing his stupidity in following that ship for so long after Athex Toor the Promethium Protector and his family had ejected. It could have taken him months to search Earth for them, months he did not have, for if he was away too long he could lose control back on Quorkidellian. And then, completely by chance, his radio had picked up the news: 'MYSTERY CRAFT LANDS ON HEATH'. He had known at once what that mystery craft was. Soon he would find the key and then he would get what he wanted. He always got what he wanted. And, once he had used the promethium weapons to conquer Blix Formenta 5, he would bring his armies back here, to Earth. Zolborg Naphax liked Earth; it was green and pretty and the people were amusingly primitive. Conquering Earth would be a doddle.

8
Blue Blob

The Kuznets smiled sadly when they heard about the luminous green bone. 'That belonged to Cuddles,' Ringo explained. 'It was a bone from a Bejematho. They glow in the dark.'

'Unlucky if they're nocturnal,' remarked Oli.

'They are fast runners,' said Mr Kuznet. 'Tell us what you learnt about the laser beams?'

'They were from a very small ship,' said Oli. 'The only trace it left was a ring of scorched grass about a metre and a half wide. Could Zolborg Naphax land in a pod that small?'

'Oh, yes,' said Mr Kuznet, looking worried. 'That sounds like a VN33. It converts into an airbike.'

'What's an airbike?' asked Oli.

'Like an Earthoid motorbike,' said Ringo,

'except without wheels. It hovers above the
ground.'

'Sounds cool,' said Skipjack.

'They're awesome,' agreed Ringo. 'They go
really fast and you can do amazing stunts on
them.'

'Enough!' cried Mrs Kuznet. 'Our deadliest
enemy is hunting us down and all you can talk

about is airbikes! Oh, Mr Kuznet – how did he find us so soon?'

'He must have picked up news of our crashed pod and come down to investigate,' replied her husband. 'But that does not mean he knows for certain that we are here. We must hope he believes Colonel Carbide's story that our pod is really a weather satellite and goes off to look elsewhere.'

'Oh, I just know he won't rest until he finds us!' wailed Mrs Kuznet.

'If he gets close, you could ask Colonel Carbide to help you,' said Oli. 'He knows all about space, and he's big and scary and in the army. Besides, his lorry is one hundred per cent alien-proof, so once you get inside that you'll be safe.'

'But we would have to tell him who we were,' Mr Kuznet pointed out. 'He is a scientist – he would want to investigate us, or even experiment on us against our will.'

'You could offer to give him information if he promised to help you,' persisted Oli. 'Think what you could tell him about the universe.'

Mr Kuznet smiled at Oli. 'Thank you for trying to help, but this is something we could only do in a real emergency, if our very lives depended on it. Meanwhile we must be on guard for Zolborg Naphax. He will have supplies of blue potion like us, so he will look like a normal Earthoid. He may even take microscopic cells from someone in this town for his own potion, so that he can blend in without being noticed.'

'But wouldn't we see two of the same person going around?' asked Skipjack. 'I hope he doesn't use Slugger Stubbins. One of Slugger Stubbins is already more than enough.'

'He would have to remove the original Slugger Stubbins,' explained Mr Kuznet, 'temporarily or permanently.'

Skipjack's eyes opened wide. 'Remove, like abduct or something?'

'Possibly.'

'In that case I hope he *does* use Slugger Stubbins,' said Skipjack.

'So anyone in this town could be Zolborg Naphax?' asked Oli. 'Except one of us, obviously. Is there any way to tell?'

Mr Kuznet shrugged. 'Apart from little mistakes he might make, or uncharacteristic behaviour, the only way to tell for sure is by using the Hostility Detector.'

'Ringo,' cried Mrs Kuznet, 'you must keep the Hostility Detector with you at all times, do you hear? At all times. Oh, if we ever escape from this terrible nightmare alive it will be a miracle. Ringo, you are not to go outside this house.'

'Aw, Mum,' objected Ringo, 'you just said I'd be safe with the Hostility Detector.'

'Not safe enough. Mr Kuznet, you must tell Ringo to stay in this house.'

'But, Mrs Kuznet . . .' began her husband.

'Go on – tell him.'

Oli and Skipjack tiptoed out of the house.

They decided to go into town to spot Zolborg Naphax suspects. They did not expect to see Ringo for the rest of the day, but they were hardly five minutes away when they heard a whooshing noise behind them and, turning round, they saw him approaching. This was surprising enough, but even more surprisingly he was not walking, but flying, on a long board with wings.

'Wow!' exclaimed Oli. 'What's that?'

'It's a wingboard,' said Ringo as he landed beside them. The boys could see the board properly now. It was silver, pointed at the front with a slightly curved shape and painted with abstract blue patterns, like graffiti. There were blue rubber foot-bindings and the wings were like those of a bird rather than a plane, but with feathers of thin metal leaves. Ringo jumped off the board and the wings folded neatly into the sides. He picked it up and tucked it under his arm.

'See?' he said. 'Now it looks just like one of your Earthoid skateboards.'

'That is just about the coolest thing I have ever seen,' breathed Oli. 'Can I have a go?'

Ringo shook his head. 'Too risky – someone might see you.'

'And if that someone was Zolborg Naphax,' added Skipjack, 'he might think you were Ringo and suck your brain out.'

Oli was forced to accept that having his brain sucked out would be a high price to pay for a go on the wingboard. 'How did you persuade your mum to let you out?' he asked Ringo.

'I didn't,' he grinned. 'I just said I was going up for a rest and then I flew out of my bedroom window. I'm hoping Mum won't go up there for a couple of hours. Dad's on my side – he says we can't all stay hidden away for ever. Besides, you two know this town and everyone in it much better than my family – with your help we might be able to find Zolborg Naphax.'

'Have you got the Hostility Detector?' Oli asked him.

'Of course.' Ringo patted his pocket. 'We just have to look out for blue blobs.'

'What I don't understand,' said Skipjack, 'is how Zolborg Naphax can aim hostility at you when he doesn't even know what you look like as a human.'

'It's still the real me inside,' explained Ringo, 'so I'll still get the blue blobs, even if Zolborg Naphax isn't consciously aiming them at the outside me. D'you see?'

'No,' said Skipjack.

'D'you want me to go on explaining?'

'No,' said Skipjack.

'OK. So what do we do if we find Zolborg Naphax?' asked Ringo.

'We go straight to Colonel Carbide and tell him who the alien is,' said Oli.

'My money's on Mr Grimble,' announced Skipjack.

'That's just cos you'd like him to be taken away and locked up for ever in a laboratory for aliens,' said Oli.

'How did you guess?'

'Actually, Mr Grimble's a good bet,' said Oli. 'It would explain why he was so nice to us on the bus the other day. Zolborg Naphax wouldn't know that Mr Grimble hates us.'

'Here comes the alien bus driver now,' said Skipjack, as Mr Grimble's Number 11 came trundling over the horizon. 'We'll put him to the test.'

As the boys climbed on, Skipjack looked closely at the driver.

Mr Grimble glared back at him. 'What are you—' he began but he checked himself, rearranged his face into a saintly smile and said, 'Nice to see you again, boys. Welcome to my bus.'

'Thanks very much,' replied Skipjack. 'I have to say that you are looking a bit off-colour, Mr Grimble. A touch green. Do you feel at all green?' He turned round to give the others a wink.

Mr Grimble appeared to be struggling to swallow something big and sharp, like a chainsaw. Finally he said, 'It's very kind of you to be concerned but I don't feel green at all. Would you like to go and sit down now?'

'Nice try, Skipjack,' whispered Ringo as they passed along the bus, 'but Zolborgs aren't green.'

'I still don't trust him,' Skipjack murmured back. 'Switch on the Hostility Detector – let's test him.'

Sure enough, the screen showed a big blue blob.

'I was right!' cried Skipjack. 'Mr Grimble *is* Zolborg Naphax!'

'He's a suspect, at least,' said Oli. 'We should do another test to make sure. Let's ask him a question that only the *real* Mr Grimble would know the answer to.'

'A question like: "What animal are you most like, Mr Grimble?"' suggested Skipjack. 'Then if he says "gorilla" we'll know he's real and if he says "flamingo" or something, we'll know he isn't.'

'Except he wouldn't answer that at all,' Oli pointed out. 'Real or not, he'd just shout at you. We'll ask him something very sensible about buses.'

So when they reached the High Street and stepped off the bus Oli asked, 'Mr Grimble, what time does the last bus leave for Bilchester on Sundays?'

'It leaves at six-thirty,' Mr Grimble beamed. 'Is there anything else I can help you with?'

'No, thanks.' Oli jumped off and as the bus pulled away he checked the timetable in the shelter. 'Oh, blog – he's right. It looks like he's the real Mr Grimble, after all. But why is he being so nice?'

'And what about the blue blob?' added Skipjack.

'He might be aiming hostility at Ringo just cos he's with us,' said Oli.

'That's true,' Skipjack admitted. 'But we should still keep him on our list.'

They decided to park themselves on the High Street bench to see if any more blue blobs came by. Once they were settled and Ringo had rolled his wingboard under the bench so that it wouldn't attract attention, he looked at the Hostility Detector again.

'Four green blobs,' he said, 'and look – there's a blue blob too, moving off to the right.'

'That'll be Mr Grimble driving his bus away,' said Oli.

'But who are all the green blobs?' wondered Ringo.

'Well, two of them are me and Skip, obviously,' Oli told him, 'and the others must be Doctor Levity and Sid.'

It didn't seem to have occurred to Ringo that Doctor Levity and Sid would like him enough to be green blobs. He looked pleased. Then Skipjack asked for a go with the Hostility Detector and Ringo was amazed at the number of blue blobs that popped up.

'From Skipjack's point of view almost everyone in the town is a blue blob,' Oli told him.

'What I'm looking for,' said Skipjack, 'is a pink blob.'

'Ah-ha – you mean Daisy. Look, that must be Daisy.' Oli pointed to a second green blob in the direction of Doctor Levity's shop.

Skipjack shook his head. 'No, no. That must

be just a customer who happens to like me,' he said. 'Daisy's obviously not there. She's somewhere at least 51 metres away.'

At that moment the joke shop door opened and Daisy came out. Skipjack peered at the screen again.

'On second thoughts, I can see a bit of pink around the edge of that green blob,' he said. 'It's really a sort of pinkish green. Definitely.'

Daisy saw them sitting on the bench, waved and hurried over. She was the kind of blue-eyed, fair-haired girl whom advertisers of wholesome products like fruit yoghurt picked to star in their commercials, usually dancing through flowery meadows in the sunshine. With puppies.

'Hello, boys!' she squeaked. 'Isn't it exciting about all these aliens? I hope I don't meet any.'

'You might be talking to one now,' said Skipjack.

For a moment Daisy looked alarmed. Then she squealed with laughter. 'Oh, you mean *you*! You are funny, Skipjack. But you must admit it's quite scary.'

There was a terrific rumbling noise, like the approach of a whole squadron of World War II bombers. The Mobile UFO Investigation Unit turned into the High Street.

Skipjack said, 'You just stick close to Colonel Carbide, Daisy. He'll protect you.'

Daisy wrinkled her pretty nose. 'He's even scarier than the aliens. Well, I must go. Grandpa wants a bag of chocolate toffees from the sweet shop. Bye!'

She skipped away and Skipjack frowned as he watched the retreat of her unrelentingly green blob on the screen. He gave the Hostility Detector a shake. 'I don't think this is working properly,' he remarked.

'Look – Colonel Carbide's parking right outside the library,' said Oli, watching the huge lorry manoeuvring backwards and forwards. 'Miss Harbottle isn't going to like that.'

Sure enough, the library doors swung open and a large woman shot out. She wore green-rimmed spectacles and clothes that looked as if she had draped herself in them, rather than actually put them on. She was adorned with so many bracelets and necklaces that even from across the street the boys could hear her jangling like Santa's sleigh.

'You can't park here!' she announced as Colonel Carbide lowered himself from the driver's seat.

'I'm on Government Business,' he replied.

'You have to be on *library* business to park here,' she told him sternly. 'Kindly remove your lorry.'

'She's got a whole *voice*,' said Skipjack with interest. 'I've only ever heard her whispering before.'

'Whatever business you do in this library can't be as important as my Government Business,' said Colonel Carbide.

'My books are far more important than your

silly aliens!' hooted Miss Harbottle.

'Then I suggest you go back to your books and leave me and my aliens in peace.'

'I insist that you take your nasty machine away!' screeched Miss Harbottle.

'She's wasted in a library,' remarked Skipjack admiringly. 'She should be selling fish in the market or opera singing or something.'

By now the scene had attracted a small crowd

of appreciative onlookers.

'I shall count to three and then I shall call the police!' announced Miss Harbottle.

But there was no need to do this, for the police, such as they were in that small town, had already arrived.

'Now, now, now — what's all this?' said Constable Bosk, pushing his way through the audience.

Miss Harbottle would have preferred someone with a reputation for wisdom and justice — King Solomon, perhaps — and not just PC Bosk who only had a reputation for interference and bossiness. But she had little choice. 'Ah, Constable,' she said, 'I'm so glad you are here. This man has parked his lorry in the library's own space. Kindly tell him to remove it.'

'As I have told this woman,' put in Colonel Carbide, 'I am here on Government Business. My authority therefore exceeds your own authority, Constable.'

Constable Bosk was torn. On the one hand, he resented having his authority trampled on by a stranger — *and* in front of half the town.

Also it was his custom to insist at all times that the tiniest and most obscure laws were strictly adhered to. On the other hand, he was an avid science-fiction fan and had been harbouring secret hopes of a cosy chat with Colonel Carbide about extra-terrestrial life, hopes which would instantly be dashed if he decided against him now.

Ringo suddenly whispered, 'Look!'

In the suspension of hostilities over the road, during which the only activity was the not-very-interesting spectacle of Constable Bosk rubbing his chin, Ringo had taken the Hostility Detector back from Skipjack for another look. On the screen now was a very distinct blue blob.

9
Spot the Alien

'Zolborg Naphax!' exclaimed Skipjack.

'Or just another person who doesn't like me cos I'm with you,' sighed Ringo. 'Life would be so much easier if you two hadn't managed to annoy nearly every grown-up in the town.'

'Easier, but not as much fun,' said Skipjack.

The blue blob was in a position corresponding with the library, where Constable Bosk was now shooing away the crowd; it seemed that Colonel Carbide had won the battle, for his Mobile UFO Investigation Unit remained defiantly parked, in spite of Miss Harbottle's glares.

Watching the screen, Ringo frowned and gave the Hostility Detector a shake.

'Something wrong?' asked Oli.

'It's on the blink,' replied Ringo. 'The battery must be running out.'

'Have you got a spare?'

'No,' replied Ringo. 'It's rechargeable, but it needs sunlight. I've had it in my pocket too much.' They all watched as the screen flickered one last time and went blank.

'It's dead,' announced Skipjack. 'Now we'll never know who the blue blob was.'

'We can narrow it down,' said Oli. 'The only people still outside the library are Constable Bosk, Miss Harbottle and Colonel Carbide. We can rule out Colonel Carbide, obviously, which leaves Constable Bosk and Miss Harbottle.'

'My money's on Miss Harbottle,' said Skipjack at once. 'In films it's always the least likely person who's guilty. And everyone knows that librarians lead Secret Lives. Don't forget that Catwoman was a librarian and she had Batman fooled for ages.'

'But if I was Zolborg Naphax,' said Oli, 'I'd disguise myself as a policeman, so I could be out and about all the time and have more chance of tracking down the Kuznets. I wouldn't want to be stuck in the library all day. Anyway, can a male alien turn into a female human?'

'Yes,' replied Ringo, 'or even an animal, but that's really dangerous cos you can get stuck and not be able to turn back.'

'How can we find out which one of them is Zolborg Naphax,' wondered Skipjack, 'without getting de-brained?'

Oli said, 'If he's taking the same blue potion as Ringo he'll go back to looking like an alien sometime after dark. So we need to see Miss Harbottle and Constable Bosk in the middle of the night. The question is: how?'

'Wait,' said Skipjack. 'I can feel a plan coming on.' He screwed up his face in a burst of concentration. Then he cried, 'I've got it! I saw this film once, about a mad scientist who could turn himself into a monster, and there was a bit when he was being the monster and someone knocked on his door and he answered it, forgetting he looked like a monster. So everyone found out, and he was locked up in the catacombs.'

'What are catacombs?' asked Ringo.

'Dark things,' said Skipjack. 'But they aren't important. The point is: why don't we try the old ring-the-doorbell-and-run-away trick on Miss Harbottle and Constable Bosk?'

'But Zolborg Naphax wouldn't be dumb enough to answer the door looking like the real him,' objected Ringo.

'He might be,' argued Skipjack. 'The scientist was.'

'It's worth a try,' agreed Oli.

Ringo said he'd better go home before his mum discovered his absence, so the three boys left their bench and wandered down to the bus stop. Ringo took out the Hostility Detector and gave it a hopeful tap. 'I can't believe it ran out just when we might have found out who Zolborg Naphax was,' he sighed.

But Skipjack was more cheerful. 'I reckon it wasn't working properly all afternoon,' he said, 'and that explains why Daisy wasn't a pink blob.'

Less than fifty metres away, Zolborg Naphax consulted his own Hostility Detector. He wasn't looking for pink blobs. He wasn't looking for green blobs, either. He wasn't even looking for blue blobs. He was looking for purple blobs.

Purple meant fear. And on his screen he saw a purple blob. Zolborg Naphax smiled an evil smile and looked up. Exactly where the purple blob should be, three boys were getting on a bus. One of them was very afraid. The question was: which one?

* * *

After Oli and Skipjack had watched, enviously, while Ringo flew back into his bedroom, they went to discuss Skipjack's doorbell idea in the privacy of the tree house.

As they drew near Oli said, 'I hope we can get up there. Tara's been hogging it for days, trying to catch Cuddles.

Suddenly his arm was clutched by Skipjack. 'What is it?' he demanded.

'Look!' squeaked Skipjack.

Oli looked. Floating down through the trapdoor of the tree house was a luminous silver alien.

'Zolborg Naphax!' squeaked Skipjack.

The descending figure had a single leg and a huge head with big black insect-eyes and curly antennae. He landed softly on the ground beneath the tree house and then, to the boys' surprise, he fell over and lay quite still on the grass.

'He's knocked himself out,' whispered Oli. 'Perhaps we can catch him before he wakes up. I wish we had Colonel Carbide's phone number.'

A peal of laughter came from the tree house and two heads poked out of the window.

'You look so scared!' squealed Daisy.

'How d'you like our alien?' called Tara.

Recovering quickly, Oli replied, 'He's OK. We knew at once he wasn't real.'

'Rubbish,' said Tara. 'You were completely fooled.'

'He's a balloon,' explained Daisy, 'from the joke shop. Grandpa's ordered lots of alien things for the tourists and he gave us some of them to try out. We're really glad it worked on you, cos we're going to do it on real people now.'

'*Real* people?' echoed Skipjack, wondering what that made him and Oli.

The girls nodded. 'Real people with real money,' said Tara. 'We'll put up a sign saying there's an alien in our garden and we'll charge them money to see it. Don't you dare tell Mum,' she added.

Unlike his sister, Oli was not one of life's natural blackmailers. But even he could see that knowing one of Tara's secrets might be useful, so he said, 'Might tell her, might not. Anyway, we want to use the tree house now.'

'Come on, Daisy,' said Tara. 'We'll go and make the sign. How much shall we charge?'

The boys found the tree house littered with the things that Daisy had brought from the joke shop: a strange squashy creature which, when squeezed, shouted, 'Greetings from Mars', a Chinese lantern shaped like a flying saucer and two particularly unattractive green rubber masks, one of which Skipjack immediately tried on.

'Now, about tonight,' Oli began. 'One of us can go to the Police Station and one of us can go to Miss Harbottle's house. Which would you rather do?'

'Take me to your leader,' said Skipjack in his Alien Voice.

Oli looked up. 'That's a blogging ugly mask,'
he remarked. 'Well? D'you want to do the Police
Station or Miss Harbottle?'

'Neither, on my own,' replied Skipjack. 'Can't
we do them both together?'

'We'd be much quicker if we did one each,'
said Oli. 'Let's find out where Miss Harbottle
lives and then you can do whichever you're
closest to. OK?'

'Not really,' said Skipjack. He pulled the mask

off and looked at it. 'We should wear these, just in case. And we should have asked Ringo what Zolborg Naphax looks like.'

Oli shrugged. 'I guess we'll know him when we see him.'

It transpired that Skipjack lived nearest to the Police Station and so, much later that night, Oli popped on his alien mask and sneaked north and Skipjack popped on his alien mask and sneaked south.

Miss Harbottle lived about fifteen minutes' sneak away and Oli arrived to find his first problem: nowhere to hide. The librarian's front garden was really just more pavement, with a piddly little fountain in the middle and a few random pots. In the end Oli decided to hide alongside the house itself and hope that, when he peeked round at the front door to see if Miss Harbottle was an alien or not, she would be looking in a different direction. So he put his finger to the buzzer, gave it a quick press and then zoomed round the corner.

Unfortunately he zoomed straight into Miss

Harbottle's rubbish bin. Over it fell with a deafening clatter. Oli froze, not knowing whether he was safer staying still in the shadows or trying to run away. But no sign of life – Earthoid or otherwise – came from Miss Harbottle's house and he was about to creep out when a light came on next door, casting a beam right across his hiding place.

He saw that he was up to his ankles in a sea of vegetables. Miss Harbottle's bin must have been brimming with broccoli stalks, leek tops and cabbage leaves. Didn't the woman eat anything else?

'Who's there?' called a man's voice from next door.

As Oli legged it he decided that the non-appearing librarian was one of four things:

    a. a very deep sleeper;

    b. too scared to peek out;

    c. Zolborg Naphax;

    d. a rabbit.

His route home took him close to the street where Mr Grimble lived so he decided to make a small detour and double-check that this long-standing enemy, who had also been a blue blob, was genuinely the hairy old bus driver he appeared to be and not in fact a monstrous space invader.

As he tiptoed up the path towards the front door, Oli studied the passing greenery for concealment potential. One bush in particular scored a perfect 10: thick and round and within easy diving distance of the Grimble doorstep. Oli held his breath and pressed the bell.

An alarming jangle seemed to shake the whole house and, before Oli could make his break for the bush, the front door was flung open and there stood Mr Grimble.

He glared down at Oli as if he was seeing the most revolting speck of life that ever crawled out of the prehistoric slime, which he probably thought he was. Then he boomed – and Oli *felt* the boom even more than he *heard* it – '**YOU!**'

Shock froze Oli to the spot. How had Mr Grimble reached the front door so fast? Perhaps he had spent the night there. Skipjack used to have a dog that slept on the door mat to be ready for the postman's hand through the letterbox the next morning. Was Mr Grimble a postman-biter too? Finally Oli regained movement in his limbs, turned tail and ran. Mr Grimble, of course, gave chase but as he ran like a walrus with two left flippers he soon lost sight of his prey and lumbered back home, fuming.

Oli was halfway back to Pond Lane and wondering what terrible punishments Mr Grimble would demand of him and whether it would be better just to pack a bag now and run away to join the army, when he remembered that he was wearing the alien mask. Then how on earth had Mr Grimble recognised him? On the bright side, at least this meant that Mr Grimble's identification of him had been more of an instinctive reaction – a lucky guess, really – than a definite accusation that he could *prove*. Feeling more cheerful, Oli trotted home to bed.

Skipjack, meanwhile, was crouched behind the low wall in front of the Police Station wearing a long, dark coat to make himself look more anonymous. He had been crouched behind this wall for about ten minutes, trying to pluck up the courage to ring the bell. Always a nervous nocturnal adventurer, he was particularly jumpy tonight because he really didn't want his brain to be sucked out. So as well as slipping on the alien mask before leaving home, he had taken the precaution of plugging his ears with some waxy stuff that his mum used to stuff into them before his swimming lessons and he hoped that this would protect him against such a fate. But it wasn't at all hard to think up a million other things that a fearsome Zolborg could do to a puny Earthoid that were equally messy, so this was only a small comfort.

He felt relatively safe in the shadow of his wall and dreaded, once the bell-ringing was over, having to scurry home again through the open streets, for who could tell behind which corner Zolborg Naphax might be lurking? But he couldn't crouch here for ever. Even though it was obvious to him that Miss Harbottle was by far the more likely Zolborg Naphax candidate, he had to get Constable Bosk out of bed just to prove that he really was Constable Bosk.

But Constable Bosk was not in his bed. He had been out on night patrol, and at this moment he was stumping along the road towards his Police Station. He was feeling bitter and disappointed: his single reason for volunteering to tramp the streets when he'd rather be in bed was the hope of seeing another UFO, but nothing had flown about all night, not even a bat. He longed to meet a little green man who would say, 'take me to your leader', so that he could reply with authority, '*I* am our leader'. (This was not strictly true, but until Inspector Flower came back on duty in the morning it was true enough.)

As Constable Bosk approached the Police Station he became aware of something moving in the shadow of the low wall that separated the station yard from the street. As he watched, the something stood up and he could see that it was a person wearing a long, dark coat; a person who was clearly Up To No Good. He marched forward.

Skipjack, having ears plugged with waxy stuff, had no idea that Constable Bosk was bearing down on him until, just as he was reaching out to press the Police Station buzzer, a hand came down on his shoulder.

'Argh!' he yelled, turning round.

'Argh!' yelled Constable Bosk, finding himself face to face with a hideous alien.

Skipjack looked at the policeman in dismay. Even Constable Bosk wouldn't be fooled for long by a rubber mask. Any minute now it would be ripped off and Skipjack would be in more trouble than the most troublesome trouble-maker in the whole history of trouble. In a final attempt to keep up his feeble pretence, he said the first thing that came into his head: 'Take me to your leader.'

For Constable Bosk these words were absolute proof, if more proof were needed, that in front

of him stood a real live extra-
terrestrial. Pausing only to yell
'Argh!' once more and wave his arms
about in terror, he turned round and
thundered away.

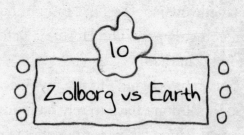

10
Zolborg vs Earth

The boys met in the Kuznets' garden the next morning to share their findings with Ringo. When Oli described the contents of Miss Harbottle's bin, Ringo shook his head. 'Zolborgs don't eat vegetables. They're strictly carnivore.'

'So in short,' summarised Skipjack, 'Miss Harbottle's too green to be a Zolborg. Mr Grimble's too like his old self to be a Zolborg and Constable Bosk is too terrified to be a Zolborg. That's it – no names left on our list of Possible Zolborgs.'

While they lay about on the grass pondering what to do next, they heard the phone ring in the house. A moment later Mr Kuznet came out.

'That was Doctor Levity,' he said. 'He has some important news. He would like you boys to go over to the joke shop now.'

'Me too?' asked Ringo.

Mr Kuznet frowned. 'Yes, but I'm not happy about you going, Ringo. The Hostility Detector is not yet fully charged.'

'But what about learning to use my own instinct, so that I don't have to rely on it any more?' argued Ringo. 'This is the perfect opportunity.'

Mr Kuznet smiled and put an arm round his son. 'Ringo, that is like saying a pool full of shankinkillers is the perfect place to learn to swim.'

'What's a shankinkiller?' asked Skipjack at once.

'Oh, it's a kind of poisonous sea-monster we have at home, with electric tentacles and seven rows of teeth. Very nasty.' Mr Kuznet sighed. 'I

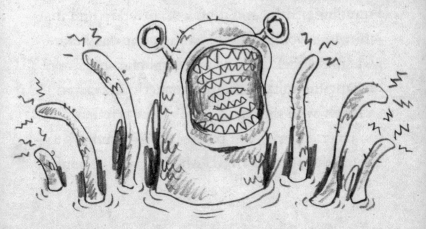

suppose that if Doctor Levity needs you to go, Ringo, then he must have a good reason.' He looked over his shoulder towards the back door. 'Go quickly, though,' he whispered. 'No reason could possibly be good enough for your mother.'

As the three boys hurried away Oli asked Skipjack, 'Why have you brought your rugby ball?'

Skipjack looked down at his hands in surprise. 'Oh, look. I didn't know I had that. It must have been automatic. Here, Ringo – you take it. It'll make you look more like an Earthoid.'

They arrived in the High Street to find Colonel Carbide's Mobile UFO Investigation Unit still parked outside the library. Of the Government Space Expert himself there was no sign but Oli noticed a dark-haired woman standing nearby and it now occurred to him that the same woman had been there the day before, when Colonel Carbide and Miss Harbottle were having their little disagreement. He wondered vaguely who she was.

Doctor Levity was pacing the joke shop floor when they arrived. 'Ah!' he cried. 'Thank the stars you're here. Come on – there's not a moment to lose.' He galloped up the narrow stairs two at a time with the boys stumbling after him, all the way to the top. Oli was expecting to be shown something through the roof-top telescope, but instead Doctor Levity opened another small door and led them into a tiny attic under the sloping eaves.

The attic was crammed with all the souvenirs of Doctor Levity's past which could not be squeezed into the shop itself: a collection of top hats, a unicycle, a stuffed warthog, a set of armoured helmets and a rolled-up oriental rug with a large label saying, 'Remember: this one *flies*.' In the midst of all this muddle was a table on which stood a large and complicated radio transceiver.

'I've been on this non-stop,' explained Doctor Levity, 'trying to make contact with someone who can take the Kuznets back to Quorkidellian. Now, while I was fiddling with the dials last night, I came across a message being transmitted from somewhere very close. I couldn't understand a word, but I managed to record most of it. This is where you come in, Ringo. See what you can make of it.'

He pressed PLAY. As soon as Ringo heard the voice he gasped, 'Zolborg!'

The others waited in silence while he listened to the whole recording. They could tell from his face that it was not good news; Zolborg Naphax clearly hadn't decided to retire from public life and take up golf. But it was even worse news than they had expected.

'He's planning to invade Earth,' Ringo told them.

'Earth?' repeated Skipjack. 'I thought he wanted to invade Blix something or other.'

'Blix Formenta 5. Not any more. He says Earth is nicer. And much easier.'

'I wish these alien dictators would make their minds up,' grumbled Skipjack.

'What else did he say?' asked Doctor Levity.

'He told his army commander to prepare troops and weapons. He also said he was close to finding the promethium key and then he'd be back to supervise the invasion plans.'

'But surely any radio waves he sends from Earth will take thousands of years to reach your planet?' said Oli.

Ringo shook his head. 'We have satellites all over local galaxies which pick up different messages and translate them into Cosmic Hyperwaves, so they've probably arrived already.'

'That's it, then,' said Skipjack. 'Earth is doomed.'

'Not necessarily,' said Doctor Levity. 'Zolborg Naphax still has to find the key and he still has to fly himself back to Quorkidellian. So the first thing we must do is get the Kuznets and the key safely away, and the good news is that I've found them a lift home.'

'That's great!' cried Ringo. 'How?'

'I've found an intergalactic bus driver who says he'll take you. He's promised to land at eight o'clock tonight, but he won't stick around for long so it's vital that we get you to the meeting point on time or he'll take off without you. I'll collect you from your house at seven-thirty. I shall ring your parents now and tell them.'

Soon after the boys left the joke shop, the local radio station received a mysterious telephone tip-off from an anonymous caller, informing them that a UFO would be landing on No-man's Heath at 8 p.m. This news was immediately broadcast and the entire town threw itself into yet another flurry of extra-terrestrial excitement, with everyone determined to be on the heath in time to witness the great event.

The boys decided to walk home, partly because

Oli was keen to avoid Mr Grimble and partly because Ringo was keen to develop his instinct to detect hostility and wanted to practise on as many passers-by as possible.

They were halfway back to Pond Lane when Oli murmured to Skipjack, 'Have you noticed that there's someone following us? *Don't* turn round!'

Too late; Skipjack had turned round. He saw a dark-haired woman wearing combat trousers and a T-shirt.

'She was waiting outside the library,' whispered Oli. 'Let's speed up – we'll try to lose her.'

But the woman would not be lost. As Oli tried to think of reasons why she might be following them he was gripped by a chilling thought: could she be Zolborg Naphax? He quickly decided not to say anything to frighten Ringo. He had to get their friend to safety, and he had to do it fast. They were close to Ringo's house by now, but if he took Ringo there he would give away the whole Kuznet family. Where could they hide?

At that moment they heard the bone-rattling

roar of the Mobile UFO Investigation Unit as
it thundered along the street and pulled up just
ahead.

That's the answer, thought Oli. Colonel
Carbide's lorry is a hundred per cent alien-proof.
He'll protect us.

He ran to big double doors and hammered
with both fists.

'What are you doing?' asked Ringo.

Oli could hear the click of the woman's
shoes as she hurried to catch up with them. He
thumped again as hard as he could. The big
doors slowly opened.

'Colonel Carbide!' gasped Oli, 'You have to
help us!' He pushed the bewildered Ringo up
the steps and into the lorry. 'That woman is
following us! We think she's a deadly alien! Jump
in, Skip – she's Zolborg Naphax!' While Skipjack
scrambled up the steps Oli glanced behind
him and saw that the woman was now running
towards them. Colonel Carbide saw her, too. He
grabbed Oli's arm, hauled him into the lorry and
slammed the doors shut. Then he turned the key
in the lock and pulled home the bolts.

Oli leaned against the doors and breathed a heavy sigh of relief. Skipjack was lying on the floor with his eyes closed and Ringo was looking utterly confused.

Seconds later they heard the woman banging on the doors. 'Johnson!' she shouted. 'Johnson!'

'Please,' Oli urged Colonel Carbide, 'you have to switch on all your alien-defence systems.'

'Johnson!' the woman shouted again. 'Open the door at once!'

'Not blogging likely,' mumbled Skipjack, still flat out on the floor.

But he was about to sit up fast. Because the next thing the woman said was, 'Johnson! This is Colonel Carbide!'

Oli would remember later that he knew the answer to his next question before he even asked it. He stopped panting and stared at the big man in front of them. 'But . . . but,' he stammered, 'if she's Colonel Carbide, then who are you?'

Smiling at them, the man brought a small bottle from his breast pocket, unscrewed it and took a swig. There was a blinding flash and through a smoky haze stepped a huge alien. In a deep metallic voice he said, 'I am Zolborg Naphax.'

11

A Quorkidellian Bug

Zolborg Naphax had the same number of arms and legs and heads as a human being, and they were arranged in more or less the same way, but his skin was red with black stripes and he was covered in slimy-looking warts. He had one large fish-eye in the middle of his high, bulging forehead, from which also sprouted a thick pair of buffalo horns. His nose was flat with four hairy nostrils, he had holes where his ears should have been and hands as huge as shovels, with black pointed claws.

As the boys shrank back against the side of the lorry, Zolborg Naphax picked up a long black gun.

'This is samarium maser,' he told them. 'Makes your insides melt. One of you is son of Athex Toor the Promethium Protector. Which one?'

None of the boys spoke. Skipjack was shaking so much he couldn't have spoken even if he had wanted to.

There was a bang on the back of the lorry. 'What's happening in there?' shouted the woman. 'Johnson! Open this door!'

Zolborg Naphax strode over to the double doors. 'I am Zolborg Naphax,' he boomed. 'Johnson is prisoner. Take message to Athex Toor. Say I have his son. And two other sons. Tell him I want key.'

There was a moment's silence. Then the woman's voice came back, less certain now. 'Where can I find him?'

Zolborg Naphax turned to the boys. 'Where?' he demanded.

Oli spoke up. 'Seven Pond Lane. It's just round the corner.'

'I'm going now,' called Colonel Carbide. Then, in an attempt to recover some of her dignity, she added, 'You will never get away with this, whoever you are.'

'You cannot stop me!' shouted Zolborg Naphax. 'You feeble Earthoid – I mighty

Zolborg! Now, go, before I shoot you through door with samarium maser!' He turned back to the boys and roared, 'Tell me who is son of Athex Toor or you all pay!'

Ringo stepped forward. Skipjack found his voice. 'Don't give yourself away, Ringo!'

'Ah-ha!' Like the Bridge Troll eyeing up the smallest Billy Goat Gruff, Zolborg Naphax took a step towards Ringo and licked his lips.

Oli turned quickly to Skipjack. 'You mustn't give yourself away either, Ringo.'

Zolborg Naphax turned round.

'Huh?' Skipjack took a moment to catch on. '*Oh!* No, I won't, *Ringo*. And nor must you, *Ringo*.'

Zolborg Naphax scowled. But then he cheered up. Keeping the samarium maser pointed at his captives, he took out his Hostility Detector. But by now fear had turned all three boys into purple blobs. He scowled again. Oli was watching him and trying to think of a way out, but the situation seemed hopeless. Not only was their captor four times their size and strength but he was also armed. They could never overpower him; their only chance was to defeat him through cunning. Meanwhile sheer terror could make Ringo give himself away at any moment. A distraction was needed. So Oli said, 'How about a game of I Spy, Ringo and Ringo? I'll start. I spy with my little eye something beginning with A.'

'Hmm,' said Skipjack, showing no surprise that his friend wanted to play guessing games while an extra-terrestrial monster breathed down their necks. 'Nope – sorry. I can't think of anything beginning with A, can you, Ringo?'

'Would "alien" count?' asked Ringo in a small voice.

'Of course!' cried Skipjack. 'Silly me. Well done, Ringo. Oh! I've got a good one. I spy—'

'Stop playing stupid game!' shouted Zolborg Naphax. He pointed the samarium maser at each of them in turn. 'One more stupid game and I shoot.'

'But who would you shoot?' asked Oli. 'Any one of us might be the son of Athex Toor and if you shoot the son of Athex Toor you will never get the promethium key. Will he, Ringo?'

Ringo and Skipjack shook their heads. 'No,

Ringo,' they said.

'Can I carry on now?' asked Skipjack. 'I spy with my little eye two things beginning with R.'

'Ringo?' suggested Ringo, who was picking up the game fast.

'Yes! Your go, Ringo.'

While Zolborg Naphax wrestled with the problem of how to work out which boys were *not* the son of Athex Toor so he could blast them to Pluto with his samarium maser, Colonel Carbide trotted along Pond Lane, looking for Number 7. How frustrating it was, she reflected, to have finally arrived in the UFO town and yet be unable to investigate because her lorry had been hijacked by a lunatic. It must have been this man, she decided, who had stolen the lorry in the first place. She and her assistant Corporal Johnson had been driving along a quiet country road two days beforehand, on their way to investigate the UFO, and had stopped so that she could fetch a notebook from the back. While she was searching she had felt a powerful electric shock pass through the whole vehicle. She had stumbled out through the rear doors and fallen into the long grass by the side of the road. Here she must have lost consciousness for several hours, for the next thing she knew it was dark and the lorry, together with Corporal Johnson, had vanished.

Quite apart from making it impossible to investigate UFOs, losing a Government Space Agency lorry bristling with expensive equipment was an embarrassing thing to do, so, instead of

reporting the loss, Colonel Carbide had set out
to find it herself. And find it she had, together
with Corporal Johnson, but matters were still
not resolved because her assistant refused to
recognise her or answer to his own name; he
appeared to have been drugged or something.
She had then noticed three boys hanging around
a lot near the lorry and had followed them to
find out what they knew. Now they had stupidly
let themselves be taken hostage. Worst of all,
yet another UFO was due to land on the heath
that very evening and if she didn't hurry up and
get this crazy kidnapper out of her lorry she
would miss that as well and with it the chance to
become the most famous UFO Investigator in
the world. It was all most inconvenient.

Colonel Carbide arrived at 7 Pond Lane
and rapped on the front door. Before long, this
opened as far as the chain would allow and a
man squinted out.

'Athex Toor?'

The man looked alarmed and shook his head.

'My name is Colonel Carbide,' she said
crisply.

'You are Colonel Carbide? But I thought—'

'I have a message from someone calling himself Zolborg Naphax,' interrupted Colonel Carbide.

Mr Kuznet gasped. 'Zolborg! Where is our son? Where is Ringo?'

'Please open this door, Mr Toor. Thank you. Zolborg Naphax has captured your son, and two other boys.

'No! This is terrible!'

'It certainly is,' agreed Colonel Carbide. 'It's *my* lorry he's holding them hostage in, together with my assistant, Johnson. He's demanding a key.'

Mr Kuznet thought fast. The simplest way to free Ringo and his friends was to hand over the promethium key, but that would condemn his beloved Quorkidellian to a future of war and bloodshed. Was there any way of rescuing the boys without such a terrible cost, and without missing the eight o'clock intergalactic bus? He glanced at his watch: 7 p.m. Could he use Colonel Carbide as an ally? No, she was clearly a woman of very little understanding. He wondered how much she knew – she certainly showed no sign of having met an alien in her lorry. So he asked, 'Who is Zolborg Naphax, anyway?'

'I have no idea,' she replied. 'I thought you knew. I only saw Johnson, but he seemed in some kind of trance. I just hope none of the equipment in my lorry has been broken.'

'Is there any way into the back of your lorry apart from through the rear doors?' asked Mr Kuznet.

'There's a glass roof which slides back,' she told him. 'That might be open, I suppose, but you'd never be able to climb up there without being noticed. Oh, when I think of all the damage he could do to my computers and weapons!' She began to count them off on her fingers: the net shooter, the sleeping-drug dart gun, the canister of Immobilising Gunge . . .

Mr Kuznet listened, and while he listened he watched an insect buzzing about in a big jar on the hall table. It was a Quorkidellian bug which had found its way into their luggage and which Ringo had caught, and now it was waiting in the hall, with their other belongings, for Doctor

Levity to collect them all in thirty minutes.

And while Mr Kuznet heard the words 'immobilising gunge' and watched the insect from Quorkidellian he was struck by a plan, a plan which involved considerable danger to

himself but which might just work.

'Excuse me,' he said to Colonel Carbide and while she continued to fuss about her equipment he quietly closed the door and went to look for his wife.

He found her standing on the back doorstep, calling Cuddles.

She turned to him, worried. 'Oh, Mr Kuznet – that silly Drongbat has run away again,' she said. 'I've been calling and calling. And he didn't come back for his lunch, either, which means that quite soon the effects of his potion will run out. Where can he be?'

Mr Kuznet took both her hands in his. 'I'm afraid we have more to worry about than Cuddles, Mrs Kuznet,' he said gently. 'You must be very brave.'

Back in the lorry, the boys were running out of things to spy. Oli had hoped to irritate Zolborg Naphax enough to throw him off guard and have the chance Do Something, but Zolborg Naphax was showing a frustrating ability to be very irritated and very on guard at the same time.

In any case, Oli had no idea what sort of Something he could Do. He could see several weapons in wall-racks, with exciting names like 'net shooter' and 'sleeping-drug dart gun', but the racks were padlocked. Oli was just looking around for anything else he could use, and was wondering in desperation whether Skipjack's rugby ball would be any good, when he noticed a small insect fly in through a gap in the glass roof. Then his attention was caught by a wail from Skipjack and, turning round, Oli saw what had given his friend such a shock: Zolborg Naphax was holding a straw.

All three boys clamped their hands over their ears and watched with mounting horror to see what Zolborg Naphax would do next.

The big alien opened a cupboard and rummaged about inside. Then he took out a can of cola, opened it, stuck in the straw and began to drink. Six hands were removed from six ears with three sighs of relief.

The insect had moved down to hover near a fire extinguisher. Now it made a beeline for Oli and as it hummed about near him Oli noticed that it was flying in a figure of eight. Then it

turned upside down in a loop-the-loop. Oli shot a glance at Zolborg Naphax, but he was busy squashing his empty can into a tiny cube. When Oli looked back at the insect it flew straight to the fire extinguisher and landed on the label.

And when Oli saw the label he realised that what he had taken to be a fire extinguisher was in fact a canister of Immobilising Gunge.

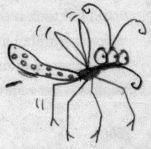

Whatever that was.

But whatever it was, it was worth trying on Zolborg Naphax. The bug now flew up to Zolborg Naphax and buzzed around his head with its volume turned up to maximum. Zolborg swatted it away but the insect was quickly back, darting about in front of him and droning like an Apache helicopter.

Oli's heart was pounding – he wanted to wait until Zolborg was completely distracted by the bug before he made his move. Oli was familiar with fire extinguishers because his science teacher, Mr Bismuth, kept a spare one in his lab for shooting ping-pong balls at children who weren't paying attention, so he had good reason to believe he could work the canister of Immobilising Gunge.

Suddenly Zolborg Naphax gave a shout of rage and reached for a nearby newspaper. He swiped at the insect, missed, swore and swiped again. Oli took his chance. He leapt to the canister, fumbled for the nozzle and fired.

A stream of orange goo shot over Zolborg Naphax, who gave a roar and lunged towards Oli.

Oli had never been so utterly terrified in all his life but he somehow kept squeezing the nozzle, praying that the Immobilising Gunge worked fast.

It did work fast. It worked very fast indeed. Zolborg Naphax was frozen mid-lunge, held fast in a rock-hard orange shell.

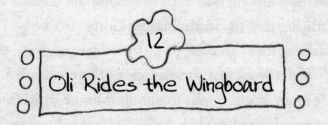

12
Oli Rides the Wingboard

Oli put down the canister with trembling hands. For a moment everyone was too stunned to speak; in fact it was Zolborg Naphax who found his voice first and let forth a foul-sounding torrent in his own language until Skipjack picked up the canister and aimed a shot of gunge over his mouth until the only part of the alien which could still move was his yellow eyeball.

'That's better,' said Skipjack. 'Oli, you were awesome.'

'*Awesomer* than awesome,' corrected Ringo. 'I've never seen anyone do anything so brave.'

'You have saved the Earth single-handed,' announced Skipjack earnestly. 'Even Batman never did that. You are officially a superhero.'

Oli looked chuffed, but slightly embarrassed, so to change the subject he said to Ringo, 'Can

Zolborg Naphax breathe with that goo over his mouth?'

'Oh, yeah,' said Ringo. 'Zolborgs don't breathe through their mouths – they breathe through those holes in the sides of their heads.'

There was a bang on the door and Skipjack opened it to find Mr Kuznet leaning against the back of the lorry, panting.

'Dad!' exclaimed Ringo. 'Look what Oli did to Zolborg Naphax! He was amazing, Dad. You should have seen him.'

'I did see him, Ringo,' said Mr Kuznet, smiling, and when the boys looked blank he added, 'Buzz, buzz, buzz . . .'

Ringo's eyes grew wide and he cried, 'That bug was *you*! What a brilliant idea! But Dad, Zolborg Naphax nearly squashed you with his newspaper – you could have been killed. And how did you know you'd be able to get back to normal?'

Mr Kuznet shrugged. 'I didn't, but the alternatives were unthinkable,' he said. 'Thank you, Oli.'

'Ringo and Skipjack were really brave as well,'

said Oli modestly.

Mr Kuznet now asked if they had seen anything of Johnson, but the boys shook their heads. In one corner of the lorry was a plastic sheet draped over something which was more or less corporal-shaped but which turned out to be a shiny black machine with a seat and handlebars.

'Zolborg's airbike,' said Ringo.

Oli and Skipjack promptly forgot all about the unfortunate Johnson while they admired the airbike. It was Ringo who found him, laid out in a sleeping compartment set into the wall, apparently fast asleep.

'So that's the man whose identity Zolborg Naphax stole,' he said, seeing the thick neck, the crew cut and the broken nose. 'Zolborg Naphax must have heard that the Government Space Expert was on the way and ambushed the lorry, but somehow he thought Johnson was Colonel Carbide and he missed the real Colonel Carbide altogether.'

'Is . . . is he dead?' whispered Skipjack.

Mr Kuznet shook his head. 'He's been comatosed – put to sleep. I know how Zolborgs do that; I can bring him round.'

While Skipjack added comatosing to his list of alien tactics to worry about, Mr Kuznet took a small phial from his pocket and held it under Johnson's nose. Within seconds, Johnson's eyes blinked open and he coughed. Then he made the mistake of sitting up and banged his head on the ceiling of his sleeping compartment.

'Eurgh,' groaned Corporal Johnson, rubbing his head.

Skipjack crossed all his fingers for 'Where am I?' because this was what people always said in films when they'd been knocked out.

'Where am I?' mumbled Corporal Johnson.

Goody, thought Skipjack, pleased.

'In your lorry,' Mr Kuznet told him. 'You've been held hostage but you'll be fine now.'

Corporal Johnson saw a very large, motionless red-and-black figure in the middle of the lorry, covered in hard-set orange goo.

'Who's that?' he asked.

'That? Oh, that's the person who held you hostage.'

'He looks like an alien,' remarked Corporal Johnson.

'That's just because you're not feeling very well,' Mr Kuznet told him. He found a drawer full of tools, rummaged about and pulled out a hammer. Thus armed, he turned to Zolborg Naphax.

'I shall remove enough Immobilising Gunge for you to get into Doctor Levity's van. If you behave, we will take you back with us. If not, we will leave you here. I am sure that when they get to know you better they will find you very interesting.' He began to chip away at Zolborg Naphax's feet.

They heard voices at the door. Mrs Kuznet, Colonel Carbide and Doctor Levity had all arrived.

'Ringo! Mr Kuznet! Are you both all right?' That was Mrs Kuznet.

'Johnson? Is the equipment all right?' That was Colonel Carbide.

'If we don't leave *now* you'll miss your bus.' That was Doctor Levity.

Mrs Kuznet and Colonel Carbide gasped when they saw Zolborg Naphax. Mr Kuznet caught his wife's eye and held a finger to his lips before she could say anything, but Colonel Carbide exclaimed,

'Is *that* the kidnapper? Why is he dressed up like an extraterrestrial?'

'He's a very sick man,' explained Doctor Levity. 'He has an alien obsession. We must take him straight back to the hospital.'

'What a completely ridiculous costume,'

remarked Colonel Carbide. She stole a quick glance at her watch: 35 minutes to go before the UFO was scheduled to land on the heath. 'Have you finished with my lorry?' she asked hopefully.

'Yes, we have,' said Doctor Levity. 'Come along, everybody.'

Holding the samarium maser, Mr Kuznet led the shuffling Zolborg down the steps while the three boys brought the airbike. They all squeezed into the camper-van: Mrs Kuznet and Skipjack with Doctor Levity in the front and everyone else in the back. Oli was given the jar containing the Quorkidellian insect to hold and studied it with interest.

'All aboard?' called Doctor Levity from the wheel. 'Off we go!'

'Stop!' shouted Ringo. 'Where's Cuddles?'

His mother put her hand on his shoulder. 'I'm so sorry, Ringo,' she said gently. 'I couldn't find him.'

It took a moment for Ringo to realise what she was saying. Then he said, 'We aren't going without him?'

'We have no choice,' said his father. 'We must

catch that intergalactic bus. Doctor Levity, please drive on.'

'No, don't!' shouted Ringo. 'I'm going back for Cuddles.' He opened the camper-van door and was on the point of jumping out when his father took hold of his arm.

'I am sorry, Ringo, but I forbid you to do this. The bus will not wait. If you miss it you will be left behind on Earth, perhaps for a very long time.'

'I don't care. Earth is fun.'

'Be sensible, Ringo. We only have enough blue potion for another few days at the most. After that you will no longer be able to hide who you really are. Do you think Earth will be as much fun then, when you are captured and exhibited as some kind of freak, or examined in a laboratory by the likes of Colonel Carbide?'

'We can't just leave Cuddles behind,' mumbled Ringo.

Skipjack gave him a pat on the back. 'Oli and I will find him and look after him, we promise.'

Suddenly Oli said, 'I think I know where he might be. Ringo, will you lend me your wingboard, for speed?'

'Of course. Just find him, please.'

Oli took the wingboard and climbed out of the camper-van. He pulled the rubbery bindings over his feet and straightened up.

'Stamp twice with your right foot to start it,' Ringo told him. 'After that you stamp to make it go faster. Use your left foot to slow down and stop.'

Oli stamped twice and the silver wings spread out. He felt the board leave the ground and put his arms out to balance himself.

'Can I take the Quorkidellian bug?' he asked suddenly. 'It might come in handy.'

'Take anything you need.' Ringo thrust the jar into his hands.

As Oli moved away he heard Ringo calling after him, 'Keep it flat and low. Hurry, Oli.'

Oli soon lost his nerves as his confidence grew. Wingboarding, he decided, was the most amazing thing he had ever experienced – he was surfing on air. He longed to fly upwards and swoop like he'd seen Ringo do, but he couldn't risk crashing and failing to bring Ringo his beloved Cuddles. So he flew sedately just above the pavement all

the way home. He passed old Mrs Higginbottom
out walking her four Pekinese dogs, but she did
nothing more than glare at him and mutter about
modern contraptions.

He parked the wingboard beneath the tree house. The trapdoor above his head was shut.

'Tara!' he yelled. There was no answer, but he knew his sister was there because he could hear thuds and bangs and whispers of 'Shhh!'

'Tara! I know you've got Cuddles up there. You have to let him go.'

'Do not! Anyway, his name's not Cuddles – it's Tripod the Second.'

Oli had expected trouble; it was time for bribery. 'I've got something to swap for him,' he called. 'A really amazing insect. Come and look.'

'I don't want an insect. I want Tripod.'

Oli tried appealing to his sister's better nature: 'Come on, Tara – he belongs to the Kuznets. They're leaving town and they'll be really sad if they can't take him.'

'They'll just have to be really sad, then.' Tara apparently had no better nature.

So he tried lying: 'They're going to Timbuktu. I'm sure they'd take you along.'

'Don't believe you.'

Oli looked at his watch. It was a quarter to eight.

Doctor Levity's camper-van was heading through the town towards Spiffing Park.

'Why is everyone hurrying in the opposite direction?' wondered Skipjack.

'Perhaps they think a UFO is going to land on the heath,' replied Doctor Levity.

Skipjack frowned. 'Why would they think that?'

'Well, someone might have told that to the radio station, to keep them all at the other end of town from Spiffing Castle.'

Skipjack grinned. 'Clever old someone!'

They were approaching the gates of the castle now, and there was still no sign of Oli. Skipjack opened and closed the gates for the camper-van to pass through, and a little way inside Doctor Levity turned off the drive into a big, flat field. They bumped over the grass and stopped by a clump of trees. Everyone climbed out and Ringo looked round hopefully for Cuddles.

Doctor Levity produced a bundle of long bamboo torches and instructed Skipjack and Ringo to set them out in a big circle so that the intergalactic bus driver would see where to land. He followed them round with a lighter while Mrs Kuznet unloaded the family's few belongings and Mr Kuznet kept watch over Zolborg Naphax.

'Now,' said Doctor Levity when everything was ready, 'we just have to wait.'

Back at the tree house there was only one option left: blackmail. Fortunately Oli had picked up a tip or two from his sister, who had been practising this for years, usually on him.

'Tara,' he said in a cold voice, 'if you don't hand over Cuddles right now, I'll tell Mum that you and Daisy have been charging people money to come into our garden and see an alien balloon.'

A long silence. Then:

'All right. But I want the bug.'

'He's all yours.'

Oli felt a little uneasy as he watched the trapdoor open, remembering the hungry eyes and slobbering jaws of the Thing. Before he had time to wonder how he would stop it from trying to escape, or how for that matter he would get it to the intergalactic bus without having chunks taken out of him, it was there beside him on the ground.

Oli took a step backwards. 'Nice Cuddles,' he cooed. 'Hurry up, Tara.'

But the Thing was not interested in Oli. It watched adoringly as Tara climbed down the ladder and as soon as she was on the ground it trotted up and rubbed its hairy orange head against her legs.

'Here's the bug,' said Oli, holding out the jar.

'Better than nothing I suppose,' she sniffed, putting it on the ground with hardly a glance. Then she saw the silver board. She took a long look and said finally, 'They aren't from Kalamistan, are they?'

Oli shook his head.

'Outer space?'

Oli nodded. Tara looked thoughtful. She stooped to pick up the Thing. 'I want to bring Tripod myself.'

Oli glanced at his watch. It was five to eight. 'You'd better hold tight, then,' he said, stepping on to the wingboard. 'We gotta fly.'

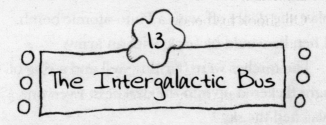

13
The Intergalactic Bus

Zolborg Naphax had been very subdued since
his capture. This was of course due mostly to
the orange gunge immobilising his mouth but
Mr Kuznet, who possessed a generous spirit and
always tried to believe the best of people (and
aliens), hoped it also meant he was regretting his
shocking behaviour and was ready to reform.

Mr Kuznet was wrong.

Zolborg Naphax was busy planning his
escape. For the past few minutes he had felt the
Immobilising Gunge soften and had realised
that it was being dissolved by the slimy secretions
produced by all his warts. He now kept very still,
biding his time until the intergalactic bus arrived.
Then, when he could take everyone by surprise,
he would snatch the samarium maser and hijack
the bus, leaving Athex Toor and his family at the

mercy of the Earthoids. He would get into the promethium store somehow, even if he had to blast the doors off with a Pluto-atomic bomb. Then he would be back, with an army.

The torches were burning well and a ring of light flickered up into the darkness. Everyone watched the sky.

'There it is!' shouted Skipjack as a triangle of lights appeared high above them.

'There it ith!' cried the oldest of Grundy Thicket's five children in the yard at Dingley Dell, where the family had gathered to look out for the UFO.

'Now we'll get them,' muttered Colonel Carbide as she and Corporal Johnson watched from the car park at No-man's Heath with several hundred others. Everyone gasped as a big silver spaceship appeared in the sky. Everyone held their breath as it hovered over the heath. Then everyone let out a cry of disbelief as it shot away.

'It's going down at Spiffing Castle!' shouted someone. 'Hurry up!' With one accord the

whole town took to its heels and charged down
the hill.

Up in the castle itself, Lord Spiffing was peering
out of the window, wondering if he should check
on his Jersey cow, Mildred, when he saw the
intergalactic bus.

'Binky, my dear,' he called to his wife. 'There
appears to be some sort of spaceship landing in
the bottom meadow.'

'How extraordinary,' replied Lady Spiffing, continuing with her sewing. 'We haven't invited anyone, have we?'

'Not as far as I know. And tourists are only supposed to come on Thursdays. It's not Thursday today, is it?'

'No, Algy. It's Wednesday.'

'In that case I think we'll just ignore it,' decided Lord Spiffing. 'I just hope they don't frighten Mildred. It's a well-known fact that cows don't like aliens.'

'Stand back, everyone!' called Doctor Levity as the triangular spaceship approached. Powerful landing lights flashed on, directing beams onto the ground that were so blindingly bright that Skipjack had to shield his eyes. Slowly and in total silence, the ship landed in the torch-lit circle. Once it was stationary the lights were switched off and everyone waited. Then, with a soft 'pshhhh', a door opened upwards and outwards and a voice announced, 'This is a request stop on the Number 11 service to Quorkidellian, calling at all planets in the Outer Spondeeling Galaxy except Blix Formenta 5, which was yesterday swallowed up by a black hole.'

Mr Kuznet turned to Doctor Levity. 'Thank you for everything you have done,' he said. 'We will never – Argh!'

Zolborg Naphax had wrenched the samarium maser from his hand. 'Hands in air,' he growled. 'Nobody move.'

They all put their hands up. Zolborg Naphax backed towards the spaceship. 'Everyone out!' he shouted. 'This is now private taxi service. Hurry up!'

An assortment of aliens shuffled off the spaceship and stood about on the grass, looking rather surprised and not altogether happy.

Zolborg mounted the steps of the ship. In the doorway he turned to face them.

'Farewell, all,' he sneered. 'I get promethium now, and I come back with army, all-powerful – Owww!'

Something had shot out of the darkness and bitten Zolborg Naphax on his great big warty leg. Something orange and hairy with very sharp fangs.

'Cuddles!' shouted Ringo.

'Well done, Tripod!' called Tara, running in from the shadows.

Zolborg clutched his leg and while he was hopping about something else zoomed in and knocked him flat. It was Oli on the wingboard. 'Get the gun!' he shouted. Mr Kuznet, who was closest, darted forwards and picked up the samarium maser.

'What were you saying, Naphax?' he said, pointing the weapon at the Zolborg's face. 'Something about being all-powerful, I believe.' Zolborg Naphax scowled. Mr Kuznet called to the passengers, 'Is there a conductor on this bus?

There wasn't just a conductor; there was a

conductor with twenty-four arms, which meant that Zolborg Naphax was kept well under control as he was marched down to the hold and locked up.

Then, while the other alien passengers climbed back on board grumbling about delays, the bus driver made another announcement over the tannoy: 'This intergalactic bus Number 11 will be departing for the Outer Spondeeling Galaxy in precisely 20 Quorkidellian seconds.'

'How long is a Quorkidellian second?' asked Skipjack.

'Three Earthoid seconds,' replied Ringo, 'so we've got one minute. Goodbye, Skipjack. Goodbye, Oli. Thanks for everything.' They shook hands, suddenly rather embarrassed.

'Here, take this.' Skipjack thrust his rugby ball at Ringo.

'Thanks.' Ringo fumbled in his bag and produced the Hostility Detector. 'This is for you, Skipjack. Good luck with the pink blobs. And Oli – you must keep the wingboard. You've earned it.'

Oli's face lit up. 'Wow, Ringo – you're a star. I

suppose it's no use saying keep in touch?'

'Don't worry,' grinned Ringo. 'I'll be back.'

'Hurry up, hurry up!' cried Mrs Kuznet, pushing Ringo towards the door. 'That driver will leave without us, I know he will. He's a Splodmosh and they are always so impatient. Make him hurry up, Mr Kuznet!'

Tara gave the Thing one last hug and then all the Kuznets climbed aboard the intergalactic bus and stood waving until the door slid shut.

Then the spaceship rose silently until it was high in the sky, hovered for a moment, and zoomed away so fast that in a flash it was gone.

And back in the Spiffings' field one small bunch of Earthoids was left behind and feeling sad. So Doctor Levity said the only thing anyone could possibly have said to cheer them all up.

'Who'd like to come to Sid's Café for a Cosmic Pizza?'

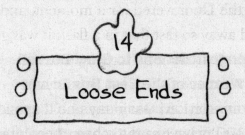

14
Loose Ends

Note delivered to Doctor Levity at the joke shop, in an envelope marked 'TOP SECRET':

Dear Doctor Levity,
I've changed my mind about
Africa – I want to go to
Quorkidellian instead. Please
can you send a message to
that intergalactic bus driver
and ask him to pick me up next
time he's passing? I've got
£7.80. Or if that isn't enough,
can he use the money to buy
me a fork-tailed Spogmondish
Drongbat?
Thank you – Tara

187

Notice seen by Mr Grumble on the Bus Station
Manager's Door:

> Congratulations to Gary Burrell
> – Winner of the Best Bus Driver
> Competition! Gary says he'll spend his
> £100 prize buying more chocolates
> for all his loyal passengers! I hope all
> our drivers will learn Gary's motto:
> Love your passengers and they'll love
> you back!

Audio CD delivered to Oli and Skipjack by
Doctor Levity:

> Hi Oli and Skipjack! Ringo
> here! I wanted to tell you
> all our news so I've asked
> Doctor Levity to record this
> message for you. Zolborg
> Naphax was arrested as soon as
> we got home and sent to the
> Black Wastes where the Dream-
> Readers have discovered that

all they have to do to get
him to be good is threaten him
with a game of I Spy. Mum's
glad to be home but I think
she misses Earth a bit, in
spite of everything - she's
stuck up lots of pictures
of Queen Elizabeth II and
she's making pizza for all
our friends. Dad's protecting
the promethium again and
helping to organise the new
presidential elections. I
took the rugby ball in on
my first day back at school
and everyone was really keen
to learn the game. Even
Dad loves it and he never
thought he'd like anything
as much as football. We've
changed the rules a bit to
suit Quorkidellian — we had
to make the ball heavier,
for instance, cos we have

less gravity than you and it
kept being kicked into orbit.
Also we play 25-aside, cos
everyone has four arms so they
can hand off three opponents
at the same time. We've
introduced some new fouls,
too, like penalties for laser-
zapping and the sin bin for
abductions. Fouls are pretty
rare though, cos the ref is a
Splodmosh and they have eyes
in the back of their head.
I hope everything's great
with you two. Did you ever
see the pink blob, Skipjack?
And have you looped the loop
on the wingboard yet, Oli?
Dad's going to make sure
the next Quorkidellians to
visit Earth make contact with
Doctor Levity so you can
send a message back with all
your news. And one day I'll

come back myself — that's a
promise.
Well, er, I think that's it.
Thanks again for everything.
Bye.

Follow Oli and Skipjack in

More Tales of Trouble!